M000203649

DAWN LEE MCKENNA'S

APPARENT WIND

A *FORGOTTEN COAST* SUSPENSE NOVEL: BOOK SEVEN

2017

A SWEET TEA PRESS PUBLICATION

First published in the United States by Sweet Tea Press

©2017 Dawn Lee McKenna. All rights reserved.

Edited by Debbie Maxwell Allen

Cover by Shayne Rutherford
wickedgoodbookcovers.com

Interior Design by Colleen Sheehan
wdrbookdesign.com

For Becky Jones
My best friend, and still my favorite Plan B

CHAPTER ONE

The old hotel was painted a shade of lavender that most places couldn't get away with, but in the quaint little coastal town of Apalachicola, FL, it fit right in.

Apalachicola is a tiny town of fewer than twenty-five hundred residents, nestled along the Gulf in the Florida Panhandle. The Apalachicola River Inn is perched along Scipio Creek, right where the Apalachicola River opens into the bay, and the bay seeps into the Gulf.

It was the kind of place that old Floridians and old tourists loved; a throwback to a time before Disney. There were two stories of clean but dated rooms, all of which overlooked the water. Guests sat on their pastel Adirondack chairs and watched the gulls follow the oyster skiffs in to the docks behind Boss Oyster next door. They had a few cocktails in the laid-back bar on the second floor of the hotel, and they enjoyed a full breakfast at Caroline's, the hotel restaurant.

Caroline's was in the back, overlooking Scipio Creek. Guests could sit inside, or they could eat on the screened-in porch right on the dock. This was where the ten or twelve board members of the Apalachicola Garden Club had gathered, to eat Caroline's wonderful French toast and talk about their upcoming fundraiser for the community vegetable garden.

There were only two other parties eating in the outdoor dining area, both of them older couples from states further north.

Awaiting the delivery of their French toast or oyster omelets, three of the board members wandered out to the dock to have a smoke. Andrea Marshall was the head of the Garden Club, a sallow, thin woman in her fifties. She whipped out her electronic cigarette and started sucking on it like it was a steroid inhaler.

Peter Winn, a slim red-headed man in his forties, owned a local restaurant and was one of the chief contributors to the community garden project, excited about purchasing local produce from its bounty. He lit a Newport menthol, his views on healthy eating somewhat more developed than his views on healthy living all-around.

The third person was Robert, who, with his long-time partner William, owned the local flower shop. It was Robert and William who had begun the community garden project and sponsored the fundraising brunch. Robert was a tall, muscular, dark-haired man in his forties. He didn't smoke, but he was in the middle of a conversation with Peter about starting a CSA from the garden, and he accompanied the other two onto the dock.

William smoked like a chimney, but he was certain the breakfast orders would be mixed up if he left the table, so he remained on the screened porch. Robert could feel him peering through the screen, resenting the fact that Robert, who needed no nicotine, was at liberty to get a nice secondhand hit anyway.

Peter exhaled a mouthful of smoke and grinned at Andrea. "You know, you can smoke that thing at the outside tables," he said.

Andrea shrugged one of her pointy shoulders. "It doesn't feel right," she said. "I'm used to smoking outside, anyway."

It was well into November. The air was dry, and the breeze off the water was a good one. It was a beautiful fall morning in northern Florida, right up until the moment that the dead woman's head started thumping up against the old wooden piling.

Standing back a few feet from the dock's edge, the small group didn't immediately see the source of the thumping, but Robert and Peter both glanced in the general direction of the edge.

"Mullet," Andrea said as she exhaled a plume of vapor.

"In here?" Peter asked without much interest.

There was a noticeable amount of slow swishing taking place in the water below the restaurant, and a couple of seagulls landed on the two nearest pilings, their feathers ruffling in the wind. There were nails tapped into the tops of the pilings to discourage the gulls from roosting there. The gulls found that amusing, and were careful where they placed their little feet upon landing. They tilted their heads and eyeballed the water beneath the restaurant.

"Anyway," Robert said, as though he'd never paused. "I think if we can get that spot at the end of Water Street, which is doing nothing for the community at the moment, then we'd have enough space to consider growing for a CSA."

"Isn't it for sale?" Peter asked.

"No, the one at the very end," Robert said. "The town owns it."

Peter nodded, then frowned as the thumping and swishing intensified beneath his feet. "That's gotta be a whole school of mullet," he said with moderate interest.

Andrea was the closest to the edge of the dock, and she leaned over as Peter and Robert stepped forward.

Andrea's scream wasn't immediate; she took some time to work up to it. There were one or two great gulps of air before she let fly with an actual screech. By then, the two men were at the edge, and peered over the side.

"Oh, crap!" Peter said, his cigarette dropping from his mouth and into the water, no more than six inches from the dead woman's face.

"What goes on?" William yelled from the other side of the screen.

Robert looked over his shoulder. William was standing up from the table.

"Nothing!" he yelled back. "Stay there!"

"If it's nothing, why should I stay here?" William called back.

By this time, Andrea had backed away from the edge of the dock, and she bolted for the main building, a hand over her mouth.

"Robert! What have you done?" William called.

"Be quiet, William!" Robert yelled over his shoulder. Despite the coolness of the day, beads of sweat had materialized on his forehead. He looked behind him again to see the other diners beginning to stand up from their chairs. He looked back down at the water and willed the woman to float back under the building before everyone saw her.

"It's a body!" Peter yelled out as he pulled his phone from his pants pocket.

"A what?" William yelled angrily. Several of the other men and women gasped or echoed William's words.

Just then, the swishing noise recommenced, and Robert's mouth fell open as the woman's head emerged fully from beneath the dock, followed immediately by the rest of her upper body. At first, Robert thought she'd only looked dead, but was actually doing the backstroke. But then her torso came into view, as did the head of the six or seven-foot gator that was carrying the woman in its jaws.

"Gator!" Robert yelled without meaning to.

Peter leaned over the edge again, though not nearly as far as he had the first time. "Hello, police?" he asked, almost frantically. "There's a gator under Caroline's, with a woman in its mouth!"

"A what!?" William yelled.

Robert looked over at him. He was still standing at the table. "Just stay there," Robert said. "Everybody stay there!"

"No, she's dead already," Peter was saying into his phone.

Robert grimaced as William threw his cloth napkin down on the table. "I *told* you we should have gone to The Owl!" he said.

CHAPTER

S heriff's Office Investigator Lt. Maggie Redmond parked her black, ten-year-old Cherokee in the small gravel parking lot in front of The Apalachicola River Inn. She'd been out on the bay in the runabout when she'd gotten the call, and it had taken her a good half hour to get to the scene. She saw that two Sheriff's Office cruisers, one Apalach PD cruiser, the crime scene techs' van and medical examiner Larry Davenport had all beaten her there.

Maggie climbed out of the Jeep and fished around in her jeans pocket for a ponytail holder as the wind blew her long, dark brown hair all over her face. She found one, and pulled her hair into something approximating a bun as she surveyed the parking area. There were quite a few people collected across the street, watching the hotel. Another handful, some of them hotel employees, were gathered by the outside staircase, talking to Deputy Dwight Shultz and Mike Rumford from Apalach PD.

Maggie shut her door and headed over to Dwight. He saw her coming, and met her halfway.

"Hey, Maggie," Dwight said. Dwight was twenty-seven, ten years Maggie's junior, but they had known each other far longer than Dwight had been with the Sheriff's Office. He was a slim man, with close-cropped blond hair, a prominent Adam's apple, and a perpetually hesitant demeanor. He usually wore the khaki uniform of an SO deputy, but today he was in khaki pants and a navy polo just like Maggie's. He was carrying a department-issued tablet.

"Hey, Dwight," Maggie said when she reached him. "I see I'm the last one here."

"Well, uh, not exactly," Dwight said. "I think our new boss is headed in this direction, and Wyatt's on his way, too."

Wyatt Hamilton was the former Franklin County Sheriff, just recently moved to the position of Public Information Officer, at his request. He was also Maggie's best friend and the man she intended to marry.

"Why's Wyatt coming?" she asked. The IO didn't normally attend crime scenes.

"Uh, yeah. On account of somebody Tweeted and then somebody else Facebooked, and now Channel 5's on their way over from Panama City."

"Oh, that's wonderful," Maggie said.

"Yeah, I thought you'd appreciate that," Dwight said. "So, Wyatt's on his way to try to make this look better than it is."

"So, what is it?" Maggie asked.

"It's a dead lady that got herself carried around by a gator for a little while," Dwight answered.

Maggie frowned up at him. Maggie was only five-three, and tended to frown up at pretty much everybody. "Huh. Have we, uh, retrieved her?"

"Oh yeah. I think the gator got kindly aggravated by all the screaming and whatnot," Dwight said. "He dropped her, and we fished her up onto the dock."

"Do we know who she is?"

"Not yet. We figured we'd better let you and Dr. Davenport have your look-sees before we checked to see if anyone here knows who she is. I don't recognize her, though, and she's kind of distinctive. You know, besides the dead thing and the gator thing. I don't think she's local."

In addition to the twenty-five hundred or so residents of Apalachicola, there were a few thousand more in Eastpoint across the bridge, and just a handful of permanent residents on St. George Island. If the woman was local, chances were decent that Dwight would know her.

"All right, so give me a quick summary of what you know," Maggie said.

"Okay. So, some locals having brunch at Caroline's found her. She was under the dock. Dead already. Dr.

Davenport says she looked like she might have been strangled. The gator might have just found her, I don't know, but he really hadn't touched her. You know, much."

"I wonder if it was the same gator that used to hang out under there from time to time," Maggie said distractedly.

"Don't know. Six-footer, not real big," Dwight said. "It moved up to the marina. Fish and Wildlife's up there babysitting it."

"Okay. Anything else?"

"That's kinda it so far," Dwight said. "I've just been trying to keep those folks over there outa the way."

"Are they the people that found her?"

"No, those folks are back there by the restaurant," Dwight said. "Mitchell and Drummond from PD are talking to 'em."

"Okay. Well, let's go see what's up," Maggie said. She started for the wooden walkway that led to Caroline's and the rooms at the back of the hotel.

Dwight fell into step with her. "You want me to stay with these folks, or you want me to come with you?"

"With me," Maggie said. "The more time you spend with me, the faster you'll get promoted."

Dwight was in the process of transitioning from Deputy to Investigator. Once he was promoted, the Sheriff's Office would have a whopping three such officers. Maggie and Terry Coyle were going to appreciate that quite a bit. Dwight also deserved it. He was the first male in his family to do something other than shrimping, and he had served the SO well over the last five years.

Mike Rumford looked up as Maggie and Dwight stepped up on the wooden deck by the stairs.

"Hey, Mike," Maggie said.

"Hey, Maggie," he answered.

"Would you keep these folks back here, please? Dwight's coming with me."

"Sure thing," Mike said.

"Hey, Maggie."

Maggie looked past Mike to two women in maid's tunics, both of them clearly upset. The woman who had spoken was Brenda Cummings. She was a scrawny woman in her early sixties, with leathery skin and short red hair. Her husband Frank was an oysterman, and had been a friend of her daddy's for years.

"Hey, Brenda," Maggie said. "Sorry about all this."

Brenda shrugged in an effort to look like she was taking it better than she was. "I hate to say it, but I'm just glad I didn't find her in her room."

Maggie nodded. "That's understandable."

Maggie and Dwight continued along the wooden walkway that ran between the hotel proper and Caroline's. There was a group of about twenty people standing in front of the door to the restaurant. Two were Apalach PD, a handful were employees of Caroline's, and the rest were civilians.

When Maggie saw the group, she sighed. "Aw, crap."

"What?"

"William and Robert," she said under her breath.

"The florists?"

"This is going to be my fault somehow," Maggie said.

Back in October, William and Robert had found a forty-year old body in the wall of their shop during renovations. Maggie hadn't even been born when he'd been put there, but William seemed to hold her responsible for every crime or dead body that threatened the tourist trade.

William saw Maggie coming and perked up, and she briefly considered turning around and going the long way around the hotel. Robert tried to hold him back, but William shook off his hand. "I want a word with the little sheriff," he said.

Robert reluctantly followed his partner. Maggie and Dwight met them halfway.

"We are smack dab in the middle of a fundraising breakfast here," William said. "Nobody wants to eat their oysters and grits when they just saw a prehistoric reptile gnawing on a dead woman."

"It was unsightly," Robert said.

"Now we're all going to go out of business because alligators are eating the tourists willy-nilly," William said with a huff.

"He wasn't eating her," Maggie said wearily. "And apparently, she was already dead. He just happened to find her."

"Oh, well, that's okay then," William said. "As long as the alligators are only eating the previously murdered tourists."

"I didn't say she was murdered, William," Maggie said. "Just that she was dead. Now, if you'll excuse me, I need to go do my job."

As Maggie headed down the wooden steps to the dock, she heard William behind her. "Robert, go start the car. Nobody's going to want to finish the meeting when there are gators about."

"There's always gators around," she heard Robert say quietly.

"Not during brunch!"

On the deck beside Caroline's outdoor dining room, Larry Davenport was squatting next to a body covered with a yellow tarp. A couple of crime scene techs stood by, along with the responders that would be carting the body to Larry's morgue at Weems Memorial.

Larry was in his seventies, a tall, white-haired Ichabod Crane. He'd been a general practitioner in Apalach for almost forty years, and had even been Maggie's family doctor for a time. He'd been almost everyone's family doctor.

He looked up from his clipboard as Maggie and Dwight arrived on the dock.

"Well, hello, Maggie dear," Larry said.

"Hey, Larry," Maggie said.

She went around to stand beside Larry on the far side of the body, so she could take a look beneath the tarp without displaying the woman for the gaggle of onlookers.

"So, what do you know so far?" she asked Larry.

"Well, judging by body temp, factoring in the temperature of the water, I'd say she's been deceased since late last night or very, very early this morning. Let's say between midnight Wednesday and four this morning."

"Okay," Maggie said.

"I believe her to have been killed prior to entering the water," Larry continued. "Owing primarily to the marks on her neck and the petechiae visible underneath her eyelids."

"She was strangled?"

"I believe so, yes," Larry answered. "At the moment, I don't see anything that points to another cause of death."

"The gator didn't get her?"

"No, that definitely wasn't the case. Look here," he said, lifting one side of the tarp. Maggie squatted down next to him.

The woman's body was clothed in gray athletic shorts and a light blue tank top. No bra, no shoes. The tank top had been pulled up above the woman's waist, and there were several puncture wounds on her abdomen, but very little blood accompanied them. The punctures didn't look like they were very deep, either.

"Judging by the very small amount of blood, it's a safe bet that she was dead when the gator found her. Obviously, I'll know more later. But the fact that she's not missing any flesh tells me the gator discovered her very shortly before the witnesses did."

Maggie nodded, then took a look at the woman's face. Recognition wasn't instantaneous. She noted first that the woman's open eyes were an odd, but pretty, shade of gray. Her curly, almost black hair was cut just beneath her chin. She looked like she might be in her thirties. Maggie's first overall impression was that the woman was beautiful. Her second impression was that she knew her. She took a deep breath and then huffed out a sigh.

"I know her," Maggie said.

"I don't recognize her as a local," Larry said.

"She wasn't local for very long," Maggie said. "And it was back in the nineties."

"Who is she?" Dwight asked.

"I'm trying to remember her name," Maggie said. "It was unusual. Pretty. Started with an 'M'. I just thought of her as Numbers 1 and 3."

"How do you mean?" Dwight asked.

Maggie pulled her iPhone out of her back pocket. "She was Axel Blackwell's ex-wife. Twice."

"Aw, crap," Dwight said.

"Yeah." Maggie had grown up with Axel. He'd been her late husband's best friend since elementary school and was a shrimper, as David had been.

She pulled up her camera, took a quick shot of the woman's face. "Marisol," she remembered suddenly. "I don't remember her last name, but she was Cuban."

She stood back up and sighed, looked over at the two stories of hotel rooms, about a dozen on each floor. "I'm going to go see if she was staying here," she said. "Dwight, you stay with Larry and get down everything we know so far."

"Okee-doke," Dwight said, opening up his tablet.

Maggie walked back up the wooden steps, ignoring William and Robert's pointed looks as she passed them. She walked back out front, and approached Brenda and the other maid.

"Brenda, can you look at a picture for me?"

"Is she chewed up?"

"No. And it's just her face."

Brenda took a deep breath, let it out slowly. "Yeah, I guess."

Maggie gently pulled her a few feet away from the others, then brought up the picture of the dead woman's face. She held it so Brenda could see it.

"Do you know her?"

Brenda's eyes widened, then she looked quickly away. "I've seen her," she said, her voice hushed. "She's a guest, but I'm not sure which room she's in."

"Okay," Maggie said, closing the photo app. "Thank you. I'm sorry about that."

Brenda shrugged, then lit a cigarette with shaky hands.

"Is anybody in the office?" Maggie asked.

"Angel. But look out by the back door," Brenda said. "She's probably smoking."

"Okay. Thanks, Brenda," Maggie said.

She looked over Brenda's shoulder as a white SUV with a Channel 5 logo pulled into the parking lot, followed immediately by Wyatt's dark blue Ford F-350. She sighed. The news sometimes came in handy, but never at a crime scene.

Wyatt was out of his truck and at the SUV's side by the time its doors were opened. Maggie watched him as he talked to the two people who got out, a stocky man in a baseball cap and a blond woman that Maggie recognized as a reporter.

When he'd been the Sheriff, Wyatt had usually worn jeans and a polo, but today he was dressed in khaki trousers, a blue button-down shirt, and a tie. It was disquieting. Maggie went down the wooden steps and started crossing the gravel lot. Wyatt saw her, said something else to the news people, and headed over to her.

At six-four, Wyatt was an imposing person. Though he was two years shy of fifty, he had the build of a much younger man. The women loved him for his dimples, his thick, brown moustache, and his laughing brown eyes. The men loved him for his wit, his humility, and his general good-guy demeanor. Maggie loved him for all kinds of reasons.

"Hey," he said, as they met in the middle of the lot.

"Hey," Maggie said back.

"Come over here," he said, and took her elbow. They walked over to the lattice-covered smoking area in front of the hotel. "So, what's the story?" he asked quietly.

"We don't have a lot you can actually say yet," she answered. "I'm 99% sure I know the victim, but I want to verify that. I'm on my way to the front office to see if she's registered. One of the maids says she's a guest."

"Who do you think it is?"

Maggie sighed. "One of Axel Blackwell's ex-wives," she said.

"What's her name—Angela?"

"No, this one is from a long time ago," Maggie answered.

"Local?"

"No."

"Okay, so what do we have, besides that?"

"Some diners at Caroline's discovered her in the water underneath the dock. She was dead already, but a gator was carrying her around."

"Well, crap."

"Yeah."

"Where's the gator?"

"Up the creek a ways," Maggie answered. "Fish & Wildlife are keeping tabs on him. I'm not sure if they're planning on euthanizing him or what."

"Once it gets out, they'll have to," Wyatt said. "They always do."

"Probably," Maggie said. "Anyway, you might want to stress that she wasn't killed and eaten by the thing."

"So, is this a drowning, or what?" Wyatt asked. "She have too much to drink upstairs at the bar?"

"I don't know if she did or not," Maggie said. "But, Larry says she was most likely strangled. Sometime late last night or very early this morning."

"This is excellent," Wyatt said drily.

"Yes."

"All right, well these people are basically going to get a line of crap," Wyatt said. "We have no solid ID, her next of kin needs to be notified first anyway, and we don't have cause of death except that it wasn't gator. That's what they get."

"I don't think you're as enthusiastic about public information as the Public Information Officer is supposed to be," Maggie said.

"I never said I wanted to inform the public," Wyatt said. "I just want to hang in there until I'm good for my pension." He looked over his shoulder at the lavender walls. "Does this tie clash with the hotel?"

"Everything clashes with the hotel," Maggie answered. "But you look handsome."

"Oh, good," Wyatt said, as Maggie walked away. "Maybe I can score with the TV lady."

"It'll be a real shame about her," Maggie said over her shoulder.

"I get a little excited when you pretend to be jealous," he said to her back.

⚓ ⚓ ⚓

Maggie crossed the parking lot and went down the short, tree-shaded path that led to the back door of the hotel office. Just beyond it was the back deck of Boss Oyster, a popular restaurant which was under the same ownership. It wasn't open yet. Maggie figured that was probably a good thing.

She found Angel Brandt smoking by the back door, right next to the No Smoking sign. Angel was in her late forties, a pretty, dark-haired woman with the deeply tanned skin of an oysterman's wife.

"Hey, Angel," Maggie said.

"Hey, Maggie. This is some kinda crap, huh?" She let out a mouthful of smoke. "I moved up from Clearwater to get away from this kind of thing."

"I know. I'm sorry," Maggie said.

"Is it a guest?"

"It could be," Maggie answered. "Brenda thinks she is. Woman in her thirties, chin-length dark, curly hair? Ring a bell?" Maggie really didn't want to show her the picture if she didn't have to.

"Cuban?"

"Possibly," Maggie said.

"Crap." Angel ground her cigarette into the sidewalk with the toe of her shoe, then stuck the butt into her pocket. "Come on in, I'll pull the driver's license for you."

Maggie followed Angel into the office that also served as a lobby of sorts for the inn. Along one wall, bottles of liquor were available for sale to guests, as well as an assortment of Boss Oyster shirts and hats.

Maggie waited at the counter as Angel flipped through a small file box next to the computer.

"I checked her in a couple days ago," Angel said. "Tuesday, I think."

"Was it just her?" Maggie asked.

"Yeah. I remember because I thought that was kind of weird, you know? I mean, she's—she was really pretty."

Maggie nodded distractedly. Yes, Marisol Somebody had been beautiful.

"Here it is," Angel said, and handed Maggie a white card stapled to a folded piece of copy paper.

Maggie glanced over the card. Marisol Corzo. Maggie didn't know if she'd ever known the last name. She'd given her address as one in Tampa, and given a cell phone number. On her vehicle information, she'd listed the license plate number of a red Kia Rio. Maggie had no idea what that was. She flipped the card over and looked at the attached paper. It was a photocopy of Marisol's driver's license. The address was different, but still in Tampa. The license was three years old.

Marisol Inez Corzo was thirty-four years old, five foot seven, and not an organ donor. Maggie stared at her picture. Even the DMV couldn't take a bad picture of her. Maggie looked up at Angel.

"Do you remember anything about her?"

Angel shook her head. "Not really. I talked to her when she checked in, but she had a hard time looking up from her phone, you know? I saw her going out to her car yesterday, but that was it."

"Okay." Maggie handed the registration back to Angel. "Can you run me copies of these?"

"Sure."

"I also need her room key," Maggie said. Angel nodded, and Maggie thought she saw her shiver just a bit. "I'll be right back."

Maggie walked out the front door, walked the few steps to the edge of the parking lot. There were two red vehicles in the small lot. One was an older Volkswagen Beetle. The other was a little compact car that looked new or close to it. It was parked in one of the spots on the far end of the hotel. She'd need to wait until the news people were gone before she took a look. The last thing they needed was for the press to track the plate and release Marisol's name before they should.

Maggie walked back inside. Angel was placing a room key on top of the photocopies she'd made, It was the old-fashioned kind, with an actual key and a turquoise, diamond-shaped plastic tag.

"Did you take any phone calls for her?' Maggie asked as she picked up the key and papers.

"No, uh-uh," Angel said. "Nobody calls hotel rooms anymore, though, you know? Everybody's got a cell phone."

Maggie nodded. "Okay. I'm going to check out her room." She looked at the room key. "Tell the ladies Room 14 is off limits, huh?"

"Will do," Angel said. "It's in the back, about halfway down."

"Thanks, Angel."

⚓ ⚓ ⚓

Maggie walked back outside. Wyatt was talking to the reporter in the middle of the lot. Maggie walked behind the little news crew, glancing over at Marisol's red car as she made her way back to the walkway by the stairs.

The maids had dispersed, but she got the eagle-eye from William and Robert again as she made her way past the officers and the small crowd from Caroline's.

She stopped at room 14. Two Adirondack chairs, one pink and one lime green, sat outside the window facing the water. The curtains were drawn. Maggie turned the key and opened the door. The bed was unmade. Very unmade. The sheets were half off the bed, and the bedspread was in knots. It didn't look like Marisol had slept alone. It didn't sound like it, either. The shower was running.

Maggie pulled her Glock from her back holster and walked slowly toward the half-open bathroom door. Once she made the door, she could see a tall form through the white shower curtain. She was about to announce herself when the water was shut off. She raised her weapon as the shower curtain was slung aside, and Axel Blackwell stood there, a lit cigarette in his mouth and a can of Dr. Pepper in his hand.

He startled, but recovered quickly. "Crap, Maggie," he said around his cigarette. "I had a dream something like this when we were in high school."

Maggie lowered her weapon, let it drop against her thigh.

"Get dressed so I can kill you," she said.

"That's not how it went."

CHAPTER THREE

Maggie had told Axel that he couldn't smoke in the room, as it was a possible crime scene. She'd told him he couldn't go outside to smoke, either, as neither one of them wanted the cluster of onlookers and witnesses to see him. They'd all seen her go into room 14, and they knew whose room it was, even if they didn't the victim's name.

So Axel sat in the small upholstered chair near the window, an unlit cigarette dangling forgotten from his lips. He stared at the crack of light between the drawn curtains. Maggie leaned against the wall near the bed and stared at him.

Axel was ruggedly handsome, in that slightly scruffy, unintentional way that some men are. He was thirty-seven, the same age as Maggie, and had been shrimping since before he'd graduated high school. His skin was perpetually and deeply tanned, his eyes frozen in a permanent squint. He was six feet tall, with a slim build made muscular by daily hard labor. He wore a hat at all times, unless sleeping or showering, and Maggie thought he looked odd sitting there, his head naked and his damp brown hair poking out in all directions.

He also looked profoundly sad. With the exception of her ex-husband's burial at sea several months ago, she'd seldom seen that emotion in him.

"What are you doing here, Axel?" she asked him quietly.

He reached for the pack of Marlboros in the pocket of his denim work shirt, then seemed to remember he already had a cigarette he couldn't smoke. He swallowed.

"Marisol called me yesterday, asked me to come have a drink with her," he said quietly.

"Where?"

Axel turned to look at her. "Here. We went upstairs for a little while, then we ran over to the BP and grabbed a six-pack and some of those wine cooler things she likes," he said. He looked back at the slice of sunshine in the window and Maggie saw him swallow hard.

"What was she doing here?" she asked.

Axel shrugged slightly. "She said she was here on business."

"What kind of business?"

"I don't know, really," he said. "We were never much for conversation."

"You had to talk about something, Axel," Maggie said, irritation creeping into her voice.

"Yeah. The fact that I was single again," he said. "She asked me how business was going. How my kids were, that kind of thing."

"Did she talk to you about what was going on with her, what was happening in her life?"

"She said she was doing good," he answered quietly. "Making good money doing marketing for her boyfriend or something like that."

"Do you know his name?"

"No, I didn't ask," he said.

"So, she has a boyfriend but she asks you to her hotel for a few drinks," Maggie said flatly.

Axel looked at her, his green eyes frank. "That happened sometimes."

"What do you mean?"

He sighed, moved the cigarette to the other side of his mouth. "She had a way of popping up out of the blue," he answered. "I wouldn't hear from her for three or four years sometimes, then she'd call and ask me to come down to Tampa, or meet her halfway, in Cedar Key or somewhere." He took the cigarette from his mouth, laid it down on the little round table. "I'll be honest with you, Maggie; almost every time I cheated on one of my wives, I cheated with Mari."

"That's awesome, Axel," Maggie said. "What is it with you and this woman?"

"Hell if I know," he said.

"You get married after knowing each other, what, three weeks? Then file for divorce five weeks later, and then you celebrate your divorce from Marci by marrying Marisol again for another two months."

"She was a lot of fun to be with, as long as you weren't in love with her," Axel said.

"*Were* you in love with her?" Maggie asked.

"At some point."

"If you don't like being married, why don't you just stop doing it?"

"I do like being married," Axel said. "I just always end up being a jerk."

"Then quit being a jerk!"

"Now?" he asked her, like she'd asked him to go bungee jumping with her.

Maggie sighed. "All right, run me through last night," she said. "What time did you meet her here?"

"Around seven," he said. "I wasn't taking the boat out last night, so I was working on my nets. She called me around six, and I finished up and came over."

"And you went up to The Spoonbill?"

"Yeah. We met upstairs," he answered. He picked the cigarette back up and stuck it in his mouth.

"How long were you up there?"

Axel rubbed at his face. "I don't know, till around nine or so."

"And then you went and got some beer."

"Yeah."

"Were you drunk?"

"When we went to BP? No."

"How drunk were you once you started drinking up here?"

"I wasn't," he answered. "A little buzzed, yeah, but you know me. I have a high tolerance. Plus, I only made it through two beers, then we, uh, moved on."

Maggie looked away, her eyes passing quickly over the bed and settling on the cheap landscape above the TV. She wasn't especially comfortable talking about the sexual activity of someone she knew so well.

"Okay, so you guys have some reunion sex or whatever you guys called it. Then what?"

"I fell asleep," he answered.

"What time was that?" Maggie asked, looking back at him.

He shook his head. "Maybe twelve or twelve-thirty. I've got the kids this weekend, so I stayed up night before last. You know, so I can sleep nights for the next few days."

Axel was a night shrimper, going out around five or six at this time of year and coming back after sunrise.

"Did you argue? Fight?"

Axel waved that off. "Nah. We only fight when we're married." He sighed, took the cigarette back out of his mouth and threw it on the table. "Damn it."

Maggie stared at the top of his bowed head. Axel was sarcastic and irresponsible, and not one to show much emotion. But he'd been devastated by her husband David's death, he was a good father to his kids even though it was part time, and he'd been a good friend to her through some very tough times. They didn't spend much time together these days, but if she needed him, truly needed his help, he would be there for her. She wasn't sure how to be there for him now.

"Axel, this is really bad," she said quietly.

"I've never raised my hand to a woman, Maggie. You know that."

"It doesn't matter. You're here."

Maggie's cell phone rang. It was Dwight. She tapped the answer icon. "Hey, Dwight," she said.

"Hey, Maggie," Dwight said. "We got everybody pretty much cleared out. You know, the civilians and whatnot. I'm coming over with a key to room 15. It's unoccupied."

"Are Mike and Pete with you?" Maggie asked.

"Yeah," he answered, as Maggie heard his knock at the door.

She hung up and opened the door. Standing behind Dwight were the two guys from the crime scene unit. Maggie didn't expect much as far as forensics went. Hotels were the worst crime scenes. They were nothing *but* DNA and bodily excretions. Maggie hadn't stayed in a hotel in years.

However, despite the fact that Axel readily admitted that he'd had sex with Marisol in that room, they would need to collect evidence of it, and anything else they could find, should Axel ever be on trial. Maggie was more interested in evidence of what Marisol was doing in Apalach, and who else might have wanted to hurt her. She knew in her bones it wasn't Axel.

She let the men in, and they all bunched up near the open door.

"Hellfire, Axel," Dwight said. "I'm really sorry."

The men in Dwight's family had been shrimping with the men in Axel's family for generations. There were no six degrees of separation in Apalach; they were lucky if they could stretch it to two.

Axel nodded at Dwight as he stood, but he didn't answer.

"Dwight, take Axel next door and take his preliminary statement while we do our thing in here," Maggie said.

"Sure thing," Dwight replied. "Uh, Wyatt's still downstairs. He's talkin' to the new boss man. The new boss man got himself on TV again."

Curtis Bledsoe, appointed by the governor to be their new sheriff, had managed to insert himself into coverage of a small pot bust just last week. This made two TV appearances in the two weeks he'd been in office.

"Is the news still here?" Maggie asked.

"No, they left."

"Then what's *he* still doing here?"

"Trying to talk to Wyatt without standing too close to him," Dwight answered. "On account of it makes him look ridiculous."

Pete, a tech straight out of college, tried to hide his laugh by coughing. Curtis Bledsoe was five foot six on his best day. He made Wyatt look like Big Bird.

Maggie sighed. "Maybe he'll be gone by the time I get done here."

"Maybe he'll come up here and give you a hand," Pete said, trying not to smile.

Nobody liked Bledsoe. This was partly because, thus far, he seemed to be more politician than law enforcement officer. But it was mostly because everybody liked Wyatt so much.

Once Dwight and Axel had gone next door, Maggie and the guys did their separate things. While they looked for trace evidence of anything at all pertinent, Maggie started going through Marisol's things, looking for evidence that someone had a reason to kill her.

Marisol's cell phone, a Galaxy of some kind with a completely useless rhinestone case, was halfway under the bed. It was dead. Maggie bagged it and set it on the table.

There were two short dresses hanging in the shuttered wardrobe that served as a closet, but the rest of Marisol's clean clothes were still in the small suitcase that was sitting open on a luggage stand. Maggie went through it carefully.

There were several pairs of panties that Maggie had a hard time understanding, as they looked more like headbands than underwear. The fact that Marisol had a matching bra for each one made Maggie feel like less of a woman somehow. There were a couple of pairs of shorts and a few flowy tops, a pair of pink sandals, and some red heels. The small pile of dirty laundry near the bathroom door had been similar. If she was here on business, that business was very casual.

A large makeup bag on the bathroom sink contained nothing of note, except clear evidence that Marisol had packed more makeup than Maggie had ever owned at one time. No prescription bottles, no illegal drugs, no condoms or condom wrappers. Nothing but high end makeup and hair products.

Maggie moved on to Marisol's purse, which she found hanging up on the back of the bathroom door. A set of keys with a Kia remote and an Epcot key ring. More makeup. A wallet with her ID and one credit card. Maggie recognized the brand as one of those secured cards for people with bad credit. There were store cards from Macy's and Belk. No cash, no pictures. A few gas receipts and an appointment card for a Tampa waxing salon. It was for the following Friday. Whatever business had brought Marisol here, she hadn't been planning to stay for long.

In the bottom of the purse, Maggie found a few loose papers. One was a receipt from the local BP, showing a purchase the night before of a pack of Camels, not Axel's brand, a pack of Seagram's Coolers, and a pack of Coors. Maggie bagged it and set it aside.

One of the other papers was the torn corner of a restaurant menu. Maggie didn't recognize it. On the back was a phone number written in pretty blue cursive. It was a local number. Maggie made note of it on her phone, then bagged the scrap of paper.

A perusal of the rest of the room garnered Maggie nothing further. She picked up the labelled evidence bags containing the cell phone and car keys and walked over to Mike, the senior of the two crime scene techs.

"Hey, Mike, can you sign off on these for me?"

"Sure," Mike said, as he pulled a receipt from a binder on the bed.

"You guys are being awfully quiet," Maggie said as he filled it out. "Nothing special?"

"Not really," Mike answered. "Of course, something like a hundred different people have been in this room in the last few months. This place is crawling with skin cells, blood, semen, hair, you name it."

Maggie sighed. "You ever stay in hotels?"

"Sure," he answered. "But I bring a kit with me."

Maggie thanked him and told him to give her a call, then she headed out the door.

CHAPTER
FOUR

Wyatt was still out front, talking to one of the guys from PD and drinking a gigantic bottle of Mountain Dew. He'd removed his tie. When he saw Maggie approaching, he patted the officer on the shoulder and fell into step with her.

"Hey," he said.

"Hey. How'd the TV thing go?"

"Not as much fun as you would think," Wyatt answered drily. "She kept calling me 'Sheriff' and we had to start over."

"Where's the new sheriff?"

"Little Curtis Bedsore? He lost interest once the press moved on," Wyatt said. "Probably late for a photo op somewhere."

"I thought you said we had to be nice to him," Maggie said.

"I was being insincere."

Maggie stopped at Marisol's little red Kia.

"This your victim's car?" Wyatt asked.

"Yeah." Maggie pulled the key fob from the bag and unlocked the door. "I want to take a look before they tow it over to the office."

"Dwight told me about Axel. Where is he?" Wyatt asked, as Maggie slipped into the driver's seat. It was pushed much farther back than Maggie would have needed it.

"Upstairs in the room next to hers," she answered. "Dwight's taking his statement."

"How is he?"

"I don't know. He's not really a heart on the sleeve kind of guy," Maggie answered. She spotted the car charger plugged into a USB port and pulled the phone out of the bag. "I had no idea he was still in contact with Marisol."

Wyatt watched her plug in the phone. "So tell me about her," he said.

Maggie started the car, waited for the little charging icon to come on, then set the phone down on the center console. "I really didn't know her. She was Axel's second wife. He was only twenty-two. His first wife was Caro, a girl we went to high school with. They only lasted seven months. Then he met Marisol. He met her at some festival in Tampa and married her a few weeks later. I didn't like her."

"Why not?"

Maggie started rummaging through the center console. "I don't know. She was too sure of herself. Too confidant, in that flirty, overtly sexy way that some women are. David didn't like her either, which tells you something, since most men try to like beautiful women."

"I like you," Wyatt said. "But it's an ongoing effort."

Maggie tossed him a look as she replaced a handful of receipts and business cards that didn't immediately interest her. "I appreciate that," she said.

"So what's the deal?" Wyatt asked. "He married her twice?"

"Yeah. The first time, they made it a little over a month." Maggie opened the glove compartment and started looking through it. "They fought all the time. After they split, he married Marci, a girl from Carrabelle. We liked her. She's the mother of his two kids. But they got divorced after seven years, and a few weeks afterwards, he comes home from a trip with Marisol in tow. They'd gotten married again. This marriage lasted twice as long as the first one."

"So...what? Two months?"

"Something like that." Maggie stuck the car manuals, insurance binder and an extra car charger back into the glove compartment and snapped it shut. "A few years later, he married Angela, and they got divorced two years ago."

"Does he know he doesn't have to marry every woman he dates?"

Maggie rolled her eyes. "Believe me, he doesn't," she said. "All of the local women know he's trouble, but he's a great guy otherwise. He doesn't lack for company."

"So what were he and his ex-wife doing here together?"

Maggie shook her head. "Apparently, they had a habit of hooking up now and then. It sounds like it was a purely sexual thing. Or maybe he still loves her a little."

Wyatt sighed and frowned down at her. "What do you think happened here?"

Maggie leaned back in the seat and blew out a breath. "I don't know. But Axel didn't do this."

Wyatt took a moment to choose his words. "Look, I like Axel. And I know you're close. But if he's got some kind of emotional connection to her after all these years, after what sounds like a pretty volatile relationship, maybe something went wrong."

"No," Maggie said, shaking her head again. "Axel's too easygoing. The reason he got married so often is that the women wanted it. And the reason he got *divorced* so often is because the women wanted it. He just goes along."

Maggie picked up the phone. The welcome screen wasn't up yet. She set it back down.

"Besides, he's way too smart. If he'd done this, he wouldn't still be here," she said. "I doubt we'd even have a body." She looked up at Wyatt. "Did you know that he got into MIT?"

"Seriously?"

"Yeah. He only applied because his guidance counselor and his mom made him. But he was a math and science geek. Our junior year, he had to start taking classes at Gulf Coast State because he'd already taken everything at our school."

"So what the hell happened?"

Maggie shrugged. "Nothing. He never intended to go to college. He wanted to be a shrimper. His mom tried to talk him into being a marine biologist, but it just wasn't what he wanted. When it's in your blood, it just is. It's simple and quiet and hard. It's total dependence on the Gulf and total independence at the same time." She looked up at Wyatt. "I'd work the oyster beds if I could."

"I'd be in favor of that," he said quietly. He and Maggie had each become less enthused about the other being in harm's way.

"We'd be poor," she said.

"Whatever."

Marisol's phone buzzed and Maggie picked it up. The welcome screen was up. "I love Androids," she said. "If this was an iPhone, we'd be screwed."

She tapped open the recent calls list. Marisol had made two calls to Axel and gotten two back, both yesterday afternoon. There were several calls to females in the few days prior to her murder, and a few to numbers without names. The one call to a local landline, with an Apalach area code, got Maggie's attention. It was the same number that had been written on the scrap of paper in Marisol's room. She tapped it and put the phone to her ear.

After three rings, a pleasant, if not cheerful, woman's voice came on the line. "Sea-Fair Wholesale Distributors. May I help you?"

Maggie was stuck for a moment.

"Hello? Sea-Fair, may I help you?"

"Uh, no. Sorry," Maggie managed, then disconnected the call.

"Who was it?" Wyatt asked.

Maggie picked at one of the rhinestones on the phone case for a moment as she stared out the windshield at an azalea bush that was rustling in the morning breeze.

"Sea-Fair," she said finally.

"Oh, hell," Wyatt said, his voice tight with frustration.

"Axel said she was here on some kind of marketing trip for her boyfriend," Maggie said. "Maybe he's in the seafood business, or boats or something."

"Well, I guess you'll have to go talk to Boudreaux and find out," he said.

Bennett Boudreaux was the owner of Sea-Fair Seafood, friend and debtor to various political leaders, and Franklin County's most acknowledged criminal. Though his crimes were mostly suspected in the widest and vaguest terms.

After thirty-eight years of living in the same small town, Maggie and Boudreaux had only met the previous year, during an investigation. Against her better judgement, they had gradually developed an odd sort of friendship. That friendship had become very important to her right before it ended just a couple of weeks ago. For reasons she chose not to analyze at that moment, Maggie did not want to see him, professionally or otherwise.

Maggie drummed her fingers on the console for a moment, then grabbed the phone and charger and turned off the car. Wyatt stepped back as she got out.

"I'll have Dwight go over there," she said without looking at Wyatt.

He frowned down at her, but she pretended not to notice, closed the door, and locked the car.

"No, you will not," he said quietly. "Dwight couldn't get a straight answer out of Boudreaux if he asked him what time it was."

Maggie leaned back against the car, jingling Marisol's keys in her hand. Wyatt waited. "I'd really rather not go over there," she said finally.

She could feel Wyatt watching her, as she stared at nothing in particular in the parking lot.

"I hate it when you don't want to look at me," Wyatt said. Maggie looked up at him and blew out a breath. "You've been acting wonky for weeks. You need to talk to me."

"Yes. I've been working my way up to that," she said.

"Does it have anything to do with us?"

"No. I mean, in a way, I suppose it does. But it's not *about* us, no." She sighed. "I'm sorry, I just needed to get my head a little straighter before we talked about it."

"Am I going to be upset?"

Maggie shrugged, and something that tried to sound like a laugh came from her mouth. "This is one of those sit-down things," she said. "Do you still want to have dinner?"

"Yes, I do. I bought steaks."

"Okay. Well, Kyle's riding home with Doug on the bus and Sky's still on her campus visit at FSU, so I'll be over right after work," she said. "I just need to run home and feed the animals."

Wyatt moved to stand in front of her, put a hand on either side of her on the car roof, and leaned closer. "Try not to look so stricken," he said. "Whatever it is, I can pretty much guarantee we've had worse conversations."

Maggie tried to smile. "Yeah." She could just pick up the familiar smell of Nautilus, and when she craned her neck to look up at Wyatt, his brown eyes were close enough to crawl into.

He bent his head and gave her a gentle kiss on the mouth. "I'll see you at the office," he said, then pushed off and started toward his car.

"Why do you tease me like that?" she said to his back.

"Because it keeps you on your toes," he said as he walked away.

CHAPTER FIVE

Maggie had driven Axel to his truck at the marina, with Dwight following, and then Axel had driven himself to the Sheriff's Office across the bridge in Eastpoint to file a formal statement. Maggie knew, almost without question, that Axel hadn't done anything more wrong than meet up with a woman he probably had no business seeing. But if it came down to a legal issue, it needed to be clear that she'd followed procedure, despite their lifelong friendship.

She asked Dwight to get Axel settled in one of the two interview rooms, then went to the vending machines to get the three of them something cold to drink. She was waiting for the second Dr. Pepper to drop when her new boss, Sheriff Curtis Bledsoe, came into the break room and put a hand on his hip.

Bledsoe was in his forties, with carefully groomed strawberry-blond hair. He wasn't overweight, but he had that soft look a man gets when he thinks golf is exercise. He was in full-on Sheriff's uniform, his shoes shined to mirror quality, but it did little for him.

"What is this I hear about this guy Blackwell following you here in his own vehicle?' he asked her.

Maggie glanced at him as she picked up the Dr. Pepper, then started dropping in some more quarters. "He did," she said. "Dwight said you wanted us to bring him here for his official statement."

"*Bring* him being the operative word here," he answered.

Maggie wanted to point out that those were actually two words, but she refrained. "He's here," she said.

"He could have just taken off," Bledsoe replied.

"He didn't," she answered.

"Look, Lieutenant, if you can't follow standard procedures in this case, I'll turn it over to Lt. Coyle," he said. "I'm not especially excited about you working a case where the chief suspect is your friend."

Maggie leaned down and pulled her RC from the bin. Then she stood and tried not to look combative when she looked her boss in the eye. "With all due respect," she said without meaning it, "this isn't Orlando. Pretty much every suspect that comes through this building is related to or friends with one of us."

"Be that as it may, I require professionalism and due diligence," he replied. "T's crossed and I's dotted, am I clear?"

Maggie was torn between reciting her fifteen-year record with the Sheriff's Office or just taking out one of the man's kneecaps.

"Transparent," she said instead.

"Very good," he said. "I understand that we're all going through a transition." He gave her a small smile. "Perhaps you in particular. But the sooner we're all on the same page, the better we'll function."

"Yes, sir," she said.

"I take my position, and the confidence the governor has placed in me, very seriously," he said, sounding like he was on TV again. "I intend to be the best sheriff this county has ever had."

There was absolutely no chance of that ever being true. Maggie nodded, hoping it looked polite enough, then headed for the door.

⚓ ⚓ ⚓

An hour later, Maggie tapped the end of her pen against the edge of the interview table and watched Axel. He'd grown more tired-looking by the minute, and was slouched against the back of his chair. His Crimson Tide ball cap was pulled down low and he was staring at the floor, but the lines on either side of his mouth had deepened, and he was very still. Maggie knew it was starting to hit him. She glanced over at Dwight, who was typing into his department tablet as he leaned against the wall.

"Axel, I think you need to get a lawyer," she said quietly.

He looked up at her. "Why? I mean, other than the fact that I was there, there's no evidence I did anything to hurt Mari. I had no reason to hurt her."

"You might not think so, but you guys had an unusual relationship. Emotional," she said.

"Oh, come on, Maggie," he said quietly. "It wasn't emotional, it was chemical."

"Chemicals have a way of getting out of balance," she said.

He looked up finally, looked her in the eye. "Maggie."

"I'm not saying that I think you had anything to do with her death, Axel," Maggie said. "I'm saying, that from the outside, it looks bad."

Axel sighed and looked at the table. "Howard Fairchild is my lawyer."

"You don't need another divorce, Axel. You need a criminal lawyer."

"I trust Howard. Plus I can afford him," Axel said. "And he's got to be better than some overworked public defender."

Something caught Maggie's eye, and she saw Bledsoe peeking through the small glass window in the door. She sighed and pushed back her chair.

"I'll be right back."

She closed the door behind her, and Dwight looked over at Axel. "Axel, I'm sorrier'n hell, man."

Axel nodded, but kept his eyes on the floor. "Thanks, Dwight."

Dwight wanted to say something else, but couldn't think of anything. He turned his attention back to the tablet.

Axel quickly swiped at the moisture on his left cheek, then pulled a cigarette from his shirt pocket and stuck it in his mouth. "Am I going to get arrested if I light this?" he asked.

"Uh, you know, I think it's still legal in government buildings," Dwight said to the tablet.

"Excellent," Axel said, and fished out his lighter.

⚓ ⚓ ⚓

Bledsoe waited in the hall for Maggie, then crooked his finger at her. The gesture infuriated her when it came from anyone other than Wyatt or her father, but she swallowed it and followed him to the break room doorway.

"Charge him," Bledsoe said without ceremony.

"With what?" Maggie asked, a panicky feeling touching her stomach.

"Suspicion of murder," he answered, his expression telling her he was dealing with an idiot.

"I *don't* suspect him of murder," she said.

"The *county* suspects him of murder, Lieutenant, and you will charge him accordingly," he said. "Did you advise him of his rights?"

"Well, I didn't Mirandize him, but he did waive his right to have his lawyer here during questioning."

"Well, now you can Mirandize him," he said.

"We have no real evidence that he did anything," Maggie said.

"He was *there*. He was the only one there who knew her," Bledsoe said, his lips stretched tightly across perfect teeth. "It would appear that maybe he's the only one in *town* that even knew her."

"I knew her," Maggie said flatly.

"Did you choke her to death?" Maggie didn't bother answering. "Charge him. Let him make bail in the morning if he can, but this county will see that this office does not play favorites or turn a blind eye."

Maggie didn't even know what that was supposed to mean. It was more soundbite than logic. She folded her arms across her chest.

"That's all, Lieutenant. Redmond," Bledsoe said, then walked past her toward his office at the end of the hall. Wyatt's old office.

Maggie took a few calming breaths, then nodded in answer to Myles Godfrey's smile as he walked past her into the break room and opened the fridge. Myles was one of her favorite deputies, a thirtyish man with dark hair and black hipster glasses.

"Hey, Maggie?" he asked, leaning against the open fridge door. "You got anything in here?"

"I never pack a lunch," Maggie said. "You need some money for the vending machine?"

"No," he said, taking a brown paper bag out of the fridge. "John picked this couple up out on 98. They're in Room 2 while we wait for the shelter to call us back. They're legal, but they're just kids, and they haven't eaten in a couple days, you know?"

Maggie watched him pull a couple of plastic containers out of the fridge. He opened one and sniffed it, then closed it up again. "Mike doesn't need this tuna salad. He's got ten pounds of deer jerky in his desk drawer."

Maggie fished three crumpled singles out of the front pocket of her jeans. "Here, get them some juice out of the machine."

"Thanks." Myles took the bills and nodded at her. "I heard Bledsoe giving you a hard time," he said more quietly. "How long you give it before somebody clocks him?"

"Too long," Maggie answered. She headed back across the hall, opened the door, and gently closed it behind her. She pulled her phone out and set it down in front of Axel.

"You need to call Howard Fairchild," she said.

⚓ ⚓ ⚓

Twenty minutes later, Maggie walked Axel down the tiled hallway between two rows of holding cells. The deputy walked a few steps ahead of them. He stopped at an empty cell and swung the door open. Axel walked in, turned around to face the door as the deputy shut and locked it. Maggie put a hand on the bars and leaned in.

"I'm sorry, Axel," she said. "It's kind of late to get a bail hearing set for tomorrow morning, but maybe Howard will get lucky. If not, he can get you one for Monday."

"Do they let you out for smoke breaks around here?" Axel asked her.

The deputy, a veteran of twenty-some years with closely-cropped salt and pepper hair, piped up. "Every four hours, you go out to the yard," he said kindly. "Next one's at four. Last one at eight."

Axel nodded, and the deputy glanced at Maggie. She jerked her head just a little, and he headed toward the door. Maggie looked at Axel and sighed. He tried to smile at her.

"David would be pissed at me for this," he said quietly.

"He'd be pissed *for* you," she said.

Axel dropped his eyes to the floor "I still talk to him sometimes, out on the bay."

"Me, too," Maggie said around a lump in her throat.

"I was supposed to take Mari out on the bay tonight," he said quietly. "All the time I knew her, she would never come out with me, not even for a simple ride."

Maggie remembered. Mari's dislike of the water was one of the things that had kept her from liking the woman. "But she was going to go tonight?"

"Yeah," Axel answered. "She was the one who suggested it. I don't know. Maybe she was trying to get another chance, maybe not. Who knows with her."

"Maybe." Maggie didn't say that another chance probably wouldn't have been a better idea than the first two.

He looked up at her. "Hey, do me a favor. Call the kids and let 'em know I'm okay, okay?"

Maggie nodded. "Yeah."

He looked back down at the floor, but wrapped one calloused finger around one of hers. "We're having some kind of crappy day."

"We are," she agreed quietly.

CHAPTER
SIX

Maggie's property was almost five acres at the end of Bluff Road, about five miles outside of town. It had belonged to her grandfather on her daddy's side, and he had built the cypress stilt house in the center of the property before Gray Redmond had been born. Now it belonged to her, and one day it would belong to one of her kids.

She stopped at the mailbox at the head of her dirt road, grabbed the handful of mail, then drove almost a quarter-mile through the tall pines, Live Oaks, and fossilized cypress. Her dog Coco, half-Lab and half-Catahoula, was sitting in the gravel parking area before Maggie even pulled in. As soon as Maggie turned off the Jeep, Coco barreled over to the vehicle, smiling widely. When Maggie stepped down, Coco collapsed at her feet and turned belly up in an expression of relief and affection.

Maggie bent and rubbed her belly. "Hey, sugar," she said. "Let's go."

Coco followed Maggie to the deck stairs, stairs that Axel had helped her father replace after the last hurricane. Seeing them made her sadder than she already was. She distracted herself by looking up at the deck for Stoopid, her rooster, who should have already been coughing at her from the railing or tumbling down the stairs to admonish her for something.

He was nowhere in sight, and she unlocked the door and let herself and Coco in, then left the front door open to allow some air through the screen door. Maggie couldn't stand to be shut up, and the windows would stay open until they got a hard frost.

She dropped her purse and the mail onto the dining room table, removed her back holster and set it beside her things, then headed for the kitchen. She was halfway there when she heard Stoopid's idea of crowing from down the hall.

She walked down the hall, Coco in tow, and opened the bathroom door. Stoopid was in the sink. So was the toothpaste, which had about eighteen holes in it. There was Stoopid poop all over the hardwood floor.

He commenced to warble out some paragraph on his day, the health benefits of toothpaste or his thoughts on Maggie's astrological sign.

"No," she said, and picked him up, then dropped him over the side. He half-flapped, half fell to the floor, then preceded her out of the bathroom. She followed him as he ran down the hall, wings at partial deployment, looking like a model plane that hadn't finished drying.

When she got to the kitchen, he was chanting at the refrigerator door. Maggie opened the door, which prompted his vocal and incessant encouragement, grabbed his scrap bowl, and then led him to the front door. The screen door scraped open, and she set the bowl down on the deck. It was immediately set upon by Stoopid, who barely looked up when Maggie slapped the door shut again.

Her cell phone rang as she passed the dining room table. It was Kyle.

"Hey," she said shortly when she answered.

"Hey, Mom."

"Did you lock Stoopid in the bathroom?"

"No. Is he locked in?"

"No, but the door was shut," she said.

"He must have pushed it shut," Kyle said. "He forgets which way it swings."

"He shouldn't be thinking about which way the door swings, Kyle!" Maggie said. "He needs to start staying back outside like a real chicken."

"Mom, he keeps getting in," Kyle answered. He sounded a lot less concerned than Maggie wanted him to.

"Buddy, there's poop all over the bathroom," Maggie said. She wanted to be mad, but that was hard with Kyle. It was easier with Sky, but not nearly easy enough.

"Sorry, Mom," Kyle said. "I was the last one out this morning. I'll clean it up when I get home. But you really should check out those chicken diapers."

"Kyle, I'm not putting diapers on my rooster," Maggie said. "He's already idiotic."

"They have ones with Christmas ornaments on them, just in time for the holiday season," Kyle said, and she heard him smiling.

"Kyle."

"Okay, Mom. Well, I checked in," he said. "I gotta go. Doug's mom wants us to walk the dog."

"Okay, buddy. I love you," Maggie said as she walked into her bedroom.

"I love you more," he said, and hung up before she could come back with a retort. It was an old routine, but it never got old. The day Kyle got too mature for it, as Sky had, Maggie would park herself in sackcloth and ashes.

Meanwhile, she needed to change and get over to Wyatt's. As she undressed, Maggie thought about the conversation they were about to have. She hadn't been putting it off because of Wyatt, she'd just needed some time to figure out what she thought about it all before she tried to explain it to him. She needed time for the anger and the hurt and the feeling of being lost to dampen down a bit.

They hadn't, really, but she knew that she'd been quiet and distant and sometimes testy the last couple of weeks, and Wyatt had been patient.

She threw on a pair of jeans and a baggy, thin sweater, brushed out her hair, and headed out of the room. She stopped in the bathroom long enough to spray some perfume, a scent made with gardenia essential oil that she bought at the farmer's market, and that was all of her preparation. She wasn't much of a beauty girl; she lacked the necessary girl skills.

She stopped at the dining room table, tucked her holster into her purse, and grabbed her keys.

Next to the front door hung a picture of her and Daddy, sitting on the side of his dock and laughing into the camera. It had been taken last spring. Before she'd met Bennett Boudreaux. Local kingpin. Collector of politicians and IOUs. The man who saved her life. Tears sprang to her eyes and she blinked them away angrily.

She wanted to go back to last spring. Instead, she just went out to her car.

⚓ ⚓ ⚓

Wyatt lived in the historic district, in a small green bungalow just a couple of blocks from Lafayette Park in one direction and the bay in the other. Maggie tapped on the screen door, and Wyatt came to the door a moment later, wearing cargo shorts and one of his many Hawaiian shirts. This one was light blue, and despite the fact that she teased him about the shirts, this one was her favorite. She knew he knew that.

"Hey," he said as he opened the door for her.

"Hey," she answered.

She stepped inside, and he bent nearly in half while she stood on tiptoe and they thus managed a kiss.

"Something smells good," she said. "What is it?"

"Charcoal," he answered.

"Oh good, I was craving some yesterday," she said.

Wyatt followed her into the breakfast area at the back of the small house. The sliding doors out to the back patio were open, and the white curtains slipped back and forth along the floor in the gentle evening breeze.

"You want a glass of wine?" Wyatt asked her as he walked around the breakfast bar and into the kitchen.

"Sure," she answered. She put her purse down on the tiled bar and watched him grab a Moscato out of the fridge.

"I'm glad you want the wine, because I forgot to pick up some RC," he said as he poured two glasses.

"I don't suppose you have any sweet tea?"

"No, because I keep forgetting to get tea bags at The Pig."

"You're from Virginia," Maggie said. "How can you not have some Luzienne in the cupboard?"

"Very easily. I don't drink tea, as you well know."

"What does your mom think about that?"

"She thinks I never should have moved to Florida," he said, and held out her wine.

They both took a long drink. Wyatt watched her over his glass, and she saw him watching. He took his glass with him as he opened the fridge and pulled out a Ziploc bag of steaks in a marinade.

"I fired up the grill so the neighbors will think we cook our meat," he said.

She knew that he knew they were biding their time, and he was helping her do it. She loved him for that. She followed him out to the back patio.

"I even opened you a salad," he said. "What do you think about *that*?"

Maggie smiled as she looked at the bowl of salad on the table. Next to it were half a dozen bottles of salad dressing. "You have a lot of dressing for somebody that doesn't eat vegetables."

"I bought it all today," he said as he slapped the steaks on the grill.

Maggie sat down at the table. "It's like it's my birthday or something," she said, picking up the tongs. "Do you want me to fix you some salad?"

"Do I have a concussion I don't know about?"

"Never mind."

Maggie served herself some salad, then rummaged through the dressings until she found a creamy balsamic. She picked at the seal until she got it open, then poured a little onto her salad. Then she sipped her wine and waited for Wyatt. The aroma of sizzling steak fat made him sexier than he already was.

He flipped the ribeyes, gave them fewer than thirty seconds to warm their backsides, then slipped them back onto the plate and brought them to the table.

"So, here's the deal," he said, as he sat down and forked a steak onto each of their plates. "We can talk about work. Yours and mine. We can talk about Axel, because of course we will." He picked up his fork and knife. "This other thing, whatever it is, we'll wait till we've eaten and given the wine a chance to hit us a little." He looked at her for approval.

She swallowed, then nodded. "That sounds good," she said.

He pointed his fork at her. "Quit looking so scared; it pisses me off," he said. "Have you cheated on me?"

"No!"

"Then eat," he said.

They each had the first bites of their steak in silence, then Maggie sighed. "I arrested one of my oldest friends today," she said quietly.

Wyatt nodded as he cut his steak. "I heard," he said. "That was a dumb move on Little Curtis's part."

"He says he wants the county to know he's tough on crime or some crap like that," Maggie said.

"He's a politician. Some law enforcement guys make great politicians, but I don't know too many politicians who make good law enforcement officers."

"Nobody in the department likes him," Maggie said.

Wyatt put his cutlery down on his plate and looked at her. "Here's the thing. You guys not liking him, that can make him pretty ineffective, and that's okay with me. He's an ass, and he really shouldn't be in his position." He took a drink of his wine. "But him not liking you guys, that could be dangerous. It can make him make decisions that put you in harm's way, just because he's indifferent to you, or worse. You need to try to get along with him. Don't kiss his butt, but don't make him resent you, either. Or fear you."

Maggie nodded. "I know. We know." She took another bite of steak. When she looked up from her plate, Wyatt was frowning at her.

"We joke about it, but it really would be perfectly fine with me if you got out," he said quietly.

Maggie swallowed her steak before nodding. "I think about that some days. I've thought about it a lot today." She shook her head. "But now's probably not a good time. There are enough changes going on, enough changes coming."

"Yeah. My job. Us," he said quietly.

"Yeah," she said. "Other things, too."

"Are you gonna get around to proposing, then?" he asked her, giving her an almost gentle smile.

He had told her a few weeks back that she would have to be the one to propose, and that he would say yes. But then other things had happened, and it just hadn't been the right time yet.

"Well, yeah," she said. "I'm working on that."

"Well, when you do, be aware that I'm not going to want to putz around about it," he said lightly.

Maggie gave him a half-smile, the lighter moment lifting some of the weight from her chest. "What's the matter? You afraid of all that sexual tension you say I'm bottling up?"

He levelled those soft brown eyes at her, his impressive brows meeting in a frown, then folded his arms on the table. "I'm not the least bit scared of you," he said quietly. "I may be in my dotage, but I can take you on my worst day."

Maggie swallowed hard, the bit of steak on her fork suspended halfway to her mouth.

"We may have both preferred to save it for the honeymoon," Wyatt said. "But I have news for you. After the wedding, it's always the honeymoon."

"Okeedoke," Maggie said weakly.

CHAPTER SEVEN

Maggie and Wyatt ate the rest of their meal minus any further romantic commentary or flirting. Wyatt told her his thoughts on his first weeks as something other than an active cop, something he had been for almost thirty years. Maggie listened more than spoke, and then they moved back to her present case.

By the time they'd cleared their plates, she'd told him the scant evidence they had in the case, shared with him her sadness when she'd had to take the call from Marisol's mother, who'd been notified in person by Tampa PD. Maggie explained that Mrs. Corzo was a widow, that her son was accompanying her to Apalach in the morning. In the meantime, Maggie would follow what few leads she had, mainly Marisol's phone contacts.

They brought fresh glasses of wine back out to the patio, and sat down on the rattan loveseat that faced the yard. Wyatt turned to face her and put an arm on the back of the loveseat behind her.

"You gonna go talk to Boudreaux?" he asked her quietly.

Maggie couldn't help looking away. She focused on the two Sabal palms against the privacy fence, the sound of their fronds rasping against the wood. She swallowed. "Yeah," she said.

"Talk to me about Boudreaux," he said gently.

She looked over at him, her face suddenly warm, her eyes hot with moisture in an instant.

"I know it's Boudreaux," he said. "Just talk to me."

Maggie let out a breath, blinked a few times to clear her eyes. "The night you went to Tallahassee for the meeting with FDLE..." She drifted off, then took a breath. "Look, if I explain the whole thing, you're going to think a lot of wrong things, things that will hurt you, before I get to the point. So I'll just blurt it out there, and then explain it. Okay?"

He swallowed. "Okay."

Maggie stared back at him a moment. She had yet to say it out loud, even to herself.

"Boudreaux is my father," she said. "My biological father."

He didn't blink. She saw him swallow once, his eyes never leaving hers, and there was a kindness, or sympathy, in his eyes that undid her. She felt the tears slip down her cheeks. Wyatt reached out and gently swiped them away with a thumb. Then he sighed.

"How long have you known that?" he asked after a moment.

"Just since that night," she said.

"I had a feeling it was something like that," he said quietly.

Maggie's surprise shocked her tear ducts into shutting down. "What—Wyatt, you've always insisted he had the hots for me."

"Yeah, I know," he said. "Right up until the day we played dueling death threats over at Boss." He saw her questioning look, and took a drink of his wine before explaining. "His was just way too heartfelt for someone that just had a sexual interest. To be honest, I walked away from that table thinking that the man was actually in love with you. But then, what, the next day, Miss Evangeline said something that gave me pause for thought."

"I don't understand," Maggie said.

"At the Soda Fountain, when that kid was hassling Sky," he answered. "She said he was a fool because he didn't realize who Sky was. At first, I thought she meant because you were a cop. But somewhere between here and Tallahassee, the other thing crept into my head. That maybe Sky was something to Boudreaux."

"Why didn't you say something to me?" Maggie asked quietly.

"Tell me how I would start that conversation, Maggie," he said gently. "And what if I was wrong?"

Maggie nodded, just barely, then looked back out at the yard a moment.

"Boudreaux told you?" Wyatt asked.

Maggie shook her head. "No. Not exactly."

She heard him sigh, and she turned back around. He had drained the last of his wine. He set the glass down on the rattan coffee table.

"You know it's bothered me for a while, this connection between Daddy and Boudreaux that no one wants to give me an honest answer about," she said.

"Yes."

Maggie took a deep breath and let it out. "I really thought that maybe Daddy had done something wrong, back in '77. I thought maybe he had been Boudreaux's alibi for some reason." She took a large swallow of her wine, waited for the warmth of it to drift down her throat and into her stomach. Wyatt waited, too.

"It bugged me that Boudreaux was the one Daddy sent to help me during the hurricane," Maggie said. "It bugged me that he didn't approve of me spending time with Boudreaux all summer, but it never seemed to scare him." She looked over at Wyatt. "He should have been a little scared by that, don't you think?"

Wyatt didn't answer. It wasn't really a question.

"The day you left for Tallahassee, I was talking to Daddy about you, about our future," Maggie went on.

"Daddy said something about how you would be okay, that it didn't take a saint to raise another man's child."

She stopped, swallowed. She had rehearsed so many times how to explain it so that it made sense, so that her thoughts back then made sense. Now she was forgetting how to put it all. Wyatt just waited.

"It probably wouldn't have meant all that much to me, what he said," she continued. "Except that it freaked him out that he said it. I mean, Daddy doesn't freak out, but he just froze for a second, and he wouldn't look at me."

Maggie looked away again. An egret had landed at the far back end of Wyatt's yard, was high-stepping in circles in that slow way they did.

"I just…for the rest of that day, all kinds of little things just seemed to drift into one whole, and I couldn't make it all shut up," she said. She looked back at Wyatt. "So, after you left, I walked over to Boudreaux's."

"Okay," he said simply. "Did you ask him about it?"

"No, but he confirmed it for me anyway," she said.

"How so?"

Maggie sighed. "I pretty much insinuated that I had feelings for him, or at least I asked him if he had ever considered that that could happen." She couldn't hold Wyatt's gaze. It had been stupid, and she felt stupid telling it.

"What the hell," Wyatt said quietly.

"I know," she said to the egret.

"What if you'd been wrong, Maggie?" he asked. "What if he'd been all in favor of that?"

"Then I would have backpedaled like hell and ruined a friendship that mattered to me, whether I should have been having that friendship or not." She looked back at him. "And then I would have told you that you'd been right all along. But deep down I knew it. I just did."

She looked down at her hands, wrapped tightly around her wine glass, and took a deep breath before she looked back up at Wyatt. "I'll be honest with you. I didn't want to lose that friendship. I even spent a very nice hour or so with him, just letting him make me laugh, just forgetting everything else, because I knew one way or another, everything was about to change. And as embarrassed as I am to say this to your face, I was kind of wishing he would go for it. The friendship would still be over, but at least Daddy would still be my daddy and I would still be who I thought I was."

Wyatt's arm dropped to her shoulders and he started to pull her toward him, but she pulled back, laid her hand on his chest. "No. I'll cry and I just don't want to right now," she said.

"Okay." He pulled his arm away, rested his chin on his hand. "So how *did* he react?"

Maggie shook her head, tried to give a half-hearted laugh that came out as frustration. "He was kind." She looked back at Wyatt. "It scared the crap out of him, I could see it. He hadn't even considered the possibility that I would…whatever. But he tried very hard not to hurt my feelings."

"But he didn't come right out and say he was your father," Wyatt said quietly.

"No. But Daddy called me a few days later, wanting me to come over and talk," she said. "He was pretty adamant about it. I asked him if Boudreaux had talked to him and he said yes. At least he gave me a straight answer, but I told him I wasn't ready."

She looked over at Wyatt. "I'm just so angry. So angry. With all of them. I mean, clearly I am my mother's daughter. I look just like her. They didn't adopt me, you know what I mean?"

Wyatt nodded. "Yeah."

"She was with him, when she was supposed to be with Daddy. I'm so angry at her that I haven't been able to see her or return her calls. I guess she knows now, because she stopped calling after I talked to Daddy," she said. "I'm angry at him for not telling me a long time ago, but mostly I'm just…I can't talk to him because as soon as it comes out of his mouth it'll be real. Do you understand?"

"Yes." He picked up one of her hands. "But listen to me. Nothing important has changed."

She looked away from the concern in his eyes. It made her feel too much. But staring at the yard didn't help, either. The tears started sliding down her face again, despite her efforts, and she was suddenly very tired from trying to hide so much. She looked back at Wyatt.

"Wyatt. I'm so lost," she said quietly.

"No. You're not," he said. "I know exactly where you are."

This time, when he put a hand on her shoulder, she leaned in and rested her cheek against his chest. His strong, familiar arms wrapped around her shoulders and he kissed the top of her head.

She closed her eyes, breathed in the scents of clean cotton and autumn and warm skin, and stopped trying so hard to not need to be comforted by them.

CHAPTER EIGHT

Mrs. Corzo was a small, delicate woman, with the pale, smooth skin so many Cuban women seemed to be blessed with. Her eyes, though, were rimmed in red, and there were dark smudges and swelling below them. When she raised her head to look at Maggie, Maggie felt a weight of guilt settle on her, like someone had just stepped carefully onto her chest.

The woman's body seemed to want to make as many physical connections as possible to that of her son. She held his hand, or he held hers, and she was standing so close to him that her hip and shoulder almost blended into him. Alfredo Corzo was a good-looking, clean cut man in his late thirties, though he looked like he could still be in college. He was just a few inches taller than Maggie, slim and neatly dressed in gray trousers, a white shirt, and black tie.

"*Señora Corzo, soy* Maggie Redmond," Maggie said quietly. "*¿Habla Inglés?*"

The woman just nodded quickly, but her son spoke up for her. "Yes, she speaks pretty well," he said.

Maggie nodded at him, then held a hand out toward Dwight. "This is Deputy Shultz. We're very sorry about your daughter."

"*Gracias*," the woman answered. Maggie could barely hear her.

Maggie looked from Mrs. Corzo to her son and then back again. "This isn't a very sophisticated morgue. We don't have a camera set-up or anything here," Maggie said. She put a hand on the plate glass window beside them. "When you're ready, the attendant will open the curtain so that you can see her. You understand, though, that you don't have to do this? We can identify her without you."

Mrs. Corzo looked from Maggie's face to the covered window. "*Quiero ver*," she said quietly. "I want to see Marisol."

Maggie looked at her son. "It's okay," he said. "We'll be okay." He wrapped a hand around his mother's elbow, as though worried she might fall.

Maggie nodded, then tapped on the window. A moment later, the short black curtain slid smoothly, soundlessly open.

Marisol was lying on a regular gurney made up with clean sheets, rather than a metal table. Larry's empathy for people in mourning was one of the many things she liked about him. She had felt it herself, when David had been killed.

A bright white sheet was pulled neatly up over Marisol's neck, then folded back. The bruises were barely visible. There were several seconds of silence. Maggie watched as every part of Mrs. Corzo's face shifted just slightly, like a sand dune being rearranged by a good wind from the west. She heard a sound come from Alfredo Corzo's throat, something he swallowed and stifled, like it might intrude on his mother's pain.

"*Mi pequeña niña,*" the woman whispered to the glass.

"That's my sister," Alfredo said.

"Okay," Maggie said quietly. She gently touched the woman's arm. "*Señora* Corzo, would you like to sit down?

The woman shook her head just once, but she didn't take her eyes from the glass. One fat tear slid down her smooth cheek.

"*Mami,* do you want some water?" her son asked her.

"*Quiero ir ahí,*" the woman answered. She looked at Maggie. "I want to go in with her, *favor.*"

Maggie swallowed and nodded, then tapped on the door. Larry's assistant, Marcus, opened the door just a bit.

"Mrs. Corzo would like a minute with her daughter," she said.

Marcus, a young black man working an internship through FSU, nodded at Mrs. Corzo. "Yes, ma'am," he said. He opened the door wider. "I'm very sorry for your loss."

Mrs. Corzo nodded, then took her son's hand from her elbow, though she didn't look at him.

"*Mami*," he said quietly.

"No," she said.

Maggie and Dwight followed them in. Alfredo stood back a ways, and Maggie and Dwight stopped behind him.

Mrs. Corzo stood next to her daughter for a moment, then Maggie saw her cross herself, then lay a hand on Marisol's forehead.

"*Mijita*," she said. "*Mami siempre te ama.*"

Mommy always loves you.

Maggie turned her head and stared out the window at the empty hall. It was barely 9am. She hoped that the morning had been awful enough that the rest of the day would seem better by comparison.

⚓ ⚓ ⚓

"We're first generation, you know," Alfredo Corzo said quietly.

He sat on one of the brown vinyl couches in the small lobby outside Larry Davenport's office, both hands holding the bottle of water Marcus had given him. Dwight had gone with Mrs. Corzo to sign the necessary paperwork for taking her daughter back to Tampa tomorrow.

"My parents were boat people," Alfredo went on, staring at his water. "They came over to Miami in 1975. My mother was pregnant, but she lost the baby. She had me a few years later, and then Mari after we moved to Tampa."

Maggie nodded and waited.

He looked up at her. "Her ex-husband, Alex, you think he did this to her?"

"Axel," Maggie corrected him quietly. "No, actually, I don't. But we have to look at every possibility."

"But the paper said you arrested him," Corzo said.

"Yes. That wasn't my decision," she said. "I'll be honest with you. I know Axel quite well. If he did this, he'll be prosecuted for it. But I don't believe he did."

"If you know him, did you know my sister?"

"Just barely," she answered. "They were—they didn't stay together very long."

"No. Neither time," he said.

"Were you and your sister very close?"

"Not by Cuban standards, no," he said with a shrug. "Mari liked to do her own thing. She didn't want to be a traditional *Cubana*, you know?"

"In what way?" Maggie asked.

"She didn't want to do manual labor like our mother, but she didn't want to go to college like me, either," he said. "By the time she graduated high school, our father was gone, may he rest. He fell from some scaffolding. He was a painter."

"I see," Maggie said.

"Marisol wasn't lazy," he went on. "She was always running and going. But she liked things to be easy. She didn't want to work, but she liked nice things. So she used her looks and her personality to get people to take care of her, to give her things."

He looked up at Maggie, and she nodded. "Okay," she said.

"That sounds like she was a prostitute or something, but she wasn't," he said hurriedly. "She just didn't mind being dependent on her boyfriends. She liked living in their nice houses, letting them buy her expensive clothes. She was like a professional girlfriend, though she always thought the next guy was going to be Prince Charming."

"I understand," Maggie said, though she really didn't. "Did she have a lot of boyfriends?"

"One at a time, but a lot, yes," he answered. "She always had the next one lined up." He sat forward, his hands tightening on the water bottle. "My sister wasn't a bad person. She loved our mother. She was always bringing her expensive presents, taking her to nice places. She was very sweet to my children, respectful to my wife. I loved my sister, but she had a certain lifestyle, and it didn't make her happy. She was always smiling and laughing, but she was never happy."

"Mr. Corzo, do you know who her boyfriend is now? Was she with someone?" Maggie fished out her notebook and clicked her pen open.

"Yes, but I don't know that much about him. A man named Toby Mann. They've only been together for a few months."

"Have you ever met him?" Maggie asked.

"Just once. I didn't like him."

"Why not?"

"He's a wannabe drug lord," Corzo answered. "He has a restaurant or something, too, and he seemed to think that made him classier and more socially acceptable, but really he's just a slick young punk."

Maggie finished scribbling and frowned up at him. "How do you know he's a dealer?"

"She told me," he answered. "She hid things from my mother, but she didn't bother too much with me. A lot of her boyfriends were criminals. Dealers, mostly. She knew I'd find out, so she was usually pretty honest about it. But our mother didn't need to know."

"Why would she assume you'd find out?" Maggie asked.

"Oh, I'm sorry," he said. "I just assumed you knew. I'm the staff psychologist for the Tampa PD."

That gave Maggie pause. "No. No, I didn't know that," she said quietly. "Who was she involved with before Toby Mann?"

"A man named Gavin Betancourt. She introduced us to him last Easter." Alfredo answered. "She told our mother that he owned a lot of real estate. Maybe he did, but he also sells coke and heroin to other rich people. She left him for Toby."

"How did Betancourt take that?" Maggie asked.

"I have no idea," Corzo answered, shaking his head. "She never mentioned it."

Maggie saw his mother and Dwight coming down the hall, and she stood up. Corzo stood as well.

"Again, I'm very sorry," Maggie said. "I didn't know her well, but she was a beautiful girl."

"Yes," he said, nodding at the floor. "She would have been a lot happier if she wasn't."

CHAPTER NINE

Maggie had no trouble getting a phone number for Toby Mann from the Tampa PD. She used her desk phone to dial it, and took a long swallow of her *café con leche* as she listened to it ring. On the fourth ring, she got his voice mail.

"This is Toby," a smooth, well-modulated voice said. "Do it."

"This is Lt. Maggie Redmond from the Franklin County Sheriff's Office," Maggie said. "It's very important that I speak with you. Please give me a call back at 850-529-6552, extension 21. Thank you."

It was her third message to him that day. She hung up the phone, picked up her purse and her to-go cup, and headed down the hall.

She wasn't used to Wyatt's new location yet. He'd been at the end of the hall for ten years. Now she had to remember to turn left from her office. His new office was just a few doors down.

He was pecking at his computer, looking more normal in his SO cap and navy polo, though he'd opted for khakis rather than jeans. He looked up as Maggie walked in.

"Hey," he said pleasantly.

"Hey." She plopped down into one of the vinyl chairs in front of his desk. "How's it going?"

He swung his chair around to face her and unscrewed the cap from the obscenely large Mountain Dew on his desk. "Lovely," he said. "I'm preparing my little speech for the career fair at the middle school."

"Are we recruiting adolescents now?"

"We are if it makes us look accessible and involved," he said, then took a swallow of his drink.

"We are accessible and involved," Maggie said.

"Well, apparently we don't look it," Wyatt said. "What are you doing?"

Maggie opened her mouth to answer, but Lance Moore, a deputy with almost twenty years under his belt, wandered into the office. "Hey, Boss?"

"You can't call me 'Boss' anymore, Lance," Wyatt said.

"Okay, Boss," Lance answered. "You remember that lady that said somebody poisoned all her dogs over there in Tate's Hell last year?"

"Yeah?"

Though Tate's Hell was a state park, there were a handful of people still grandfathered in back there.

"Well, she says somebody's been sneaking around her property. She's worried about her new dogs," he said.

"Okay," Wyatt said.

"So, I'm thinking, you know, we see if maybe the rangers can take a look-see, right?"

"Well, first, what the hell are you asking me for?" Wyatt asked pleasantly. "Secondly, why are you so scared of one little old lady?"

"Well, first of all, I'm asking you because I don't have to explain the whole thing to you," Lance answered.

"But I can't give you an answer," Wyatt said. "You people have to stop trying to get me to be the sheriff."

"You're getting kinda worked up," Lance said, deadpan. "Second of all, I'm not scared of her for no reason, Wyatt. She shot sandbags at my ass."

"They hurt," Wyatt said.

"They do."

"But if she called you, I can't tell you to pass it off to the rangers," Wyatt said. "You need to saunter down the hall and ask the sheriff."

Dwight walked in as Wyatt finished speaking, and raised a hand to Wyatt.

"Hey, Boss," Dwight said.

"Quit it, Dwight," Wyatt replied.

"Can I take Dwight with me?" Lance asked.

"No! And that's not my call, either," Wyatt said.

"So I can, then," Lance said.

"Uh, I'd go with you to wherever, Lance, but I gotta go with Maggie," Dwight said apologetically.

Lance shook his head, then waved disgustedly at Wyatt. "This is crap, Boss," he said, then stalked out of the office.

Dwight looked at Wyatt, who rolled his eyes at him as he took another swig of his Mountain Dew.

"What's wrong with Lance?" Dwight asked him.

Wyatt was swallowing battery acid, so Maggie answered for him. "He doesn't like our new leader."

"Who does?" Dwight asked.

"You get along with everybody. Why don't you like him? Wyatt asked.

"Mostly on account of he's unlikeable," Dwight said.

Wyatt raised his eyebrows at Maggie. "You guys need to fix this," he said.

"Why are you telling me?" Maggie asked.

"Because the guys look up to you," he said.

Maggie snorted. "There were frozen, dead frogs in my locker last week," she said.

"Aw, that was just in fun, Maggie, you know that," Dwight said. "'sides, me and Jake went out on our night off to gig them frogs."

"Am I supposed to thank you?" Maggie asked him, but she couldn't help smiling.

"I could use a Slurpee on the way over to Boudreaux's," he said.

"You headed over to talk to Boudreaux?" Wyatt asked Maggie.

"Yeah," she said, her eyes darting away from his.

Wyatt looked at her a moment, long enough to force her to look back at him.

"What?" she asked him.

"You okay?"

Dwight looked from Wyatt to Maggie, then back again.

"Yeah," Maggie said.

Wyatt glanced over at Dwight, as though he'd forgotten he was there. "Okay. Well, I'd like to be a fly on that wall," he said as he curled his Mountain Dew.

"Dwight's my fly," she said.

She got up and started out. Dwight pushed away from the wall.

"Dwight?" Wyatt said.

"Yeah, Boss."

"Do yourself a favor. Don't walk into Boudreaux's office with a cherry Slurpee in your hand, okay?"

⚓ ⚓ ⚓

Dwight didn't own enough fat cells to keep his body warm, so Maggie compromised by turning off the air and rolling down the windows of the Jeep. They rode together in silence until they got to the causeway that connected Eastpoint to Apalach.

Once they were over the water, Dwight cut his eyes over to Maggie. She felt him do it.

"So, uh, what do you think about this lady having Boudreaux's number?"

Maggie glanced over at him, then looked back at the road. "No idea," she said. "She told Axel she was working with her boyfriend, some kind of marketing for his company. Maybe he's in the seafood business."

"Okay," Dwight said.

Maggie sighed. "Dwight, we've known each other a long time. We're friends," she said. "It's okay to just spit it out."

"Uh, well, you know," Dwight said. "I don't truck with gossip much."

"I know," she said.

"But you know, stuff goes around a lot these days," he said. "About you and Boudreaux."

Maggie swallowed and nodded. "I know that, too."

He looked out his window for a moment. Out of the corner of her eye, Maggie saw his Adam's apple bob a few times as he worked up a thought.

"I do know that there's no way you're on his payroll," he said finally when he looked back at her.

"Thanks, Dwight. No, I'm not." She sighed. "We got to know each other pretty well over the summer, when I was working the foot case."

She paused as she looked off to her right, looked at Apalach's waterfront across the bridge. She could see the Riverview Inn, Boss Oyster, Boudreaux's seafood plant, the old shrimp boats docked at Riverfront Park. Her home.

"Then there was the thing with the hurricane, with Alessi's father," she said. "Boudreaux saved my life. He saved the kids' lives."

Dwight nodded. "Yeah. I get that." He looked over at her. "I mean I don't really know that whole story, but I get why you'd, you know, be friendly."

"It's kind of complicated," she said.

"Gotcha," he said, though it sounded more like he wanted to than that he actually did.

They coasted down the causeway and into Apalach's small downtown district.

"I will say this, Dwight," Maggie said. "Not all of the rumors about him are true, either."

"Good enough," Dwight said.

⚓ ⚓ ⚓

The soccer mom who manned the reception desk at Sea-Fair was less than jubilant to see two Sheriff's officers standing in her lobby. She'd seen Maggie come through more than once, and knew that Boudreaux would want to see her, but having Dwight along made the visit seem too professional for the woman's taste. Sea-Fair was a legitimate business, and a thriving one, but everybody knew that Boudreaux had a lot of sidelines. Presumably, the woman in the khaki skirt and fall-themed cardigan knew that, too.

She hung up her phone and smiled tightly up at Maggie. "Mr. Boudreaux would like me to take you back to his office," she said.

"Thank you," Maggie said.

She and Dwight followed the woman down a short hallway to what Maggie thought of as Boudreaux's "public" office, the one he used to impress visitors. She knew he more frequently worked out of a far plainer one at the other end of the building. Boudreaux was quite conscious of his public image, but he wasn't pretentious.

The woman knocked gently on the door, then opened it. Maggie saw Boudreaux stand up behind his mahogany desk. It was the first time she'd seen him since that night, and her breathing became quicker, less helpful.

"Maggie," he said quietly. "Come in. Please."

The receptionist opened the door wider, and Dwight followed Maggie in.

"Thank you, Nancy," Boudreaux said, and the woman shut the door behind her as she left.

Boudreaux looked quietly elegant, as usual, in a pair of gray trousers and a pale green button-down shirt that was so thin and finely tailored that Maggie would have worn it. His thick brown hair, with the touches of silver above the ears, was impeccably cut. Maggie wasn't close enough to smell it, but she knew his cologne would be faint and refined. But she also knew that his hands were calloused from years of working shrimp boats and oyster beds, and that he had more in common with his employees than with the politicians and society folks who liked to call him their friend.

Maggie realized that she and Boudreaux had been having a staring contest while she wasn't paying attention. His aqua eyes were fixed on her, though his face was expressionless.

Her first instinct was to yell at him. She'd rehearsed several diatribes in her head over the last couple of weeks. She swallowed the impulse to express herself.

"Mr. Boudreaux," she said politely, but tightly. "I don't know if you know Deputy Shultz."

"We've met once or twice," Boudreaux said, and held out a hand. "Deputy."

"Sir," Dwight said as they shook.

"Please have a seat," Boudreaux said, and swept a hand toward the two leather armchairs in front of his desk.

Dwight sat first. Maggie had hung back a bit, so she had to take a few steps before she could take the other chair. Ever the consummate gentleman, Boudreaux remained standing.

"May I offer either of you something cold, or some coffee?" he asked.

"No, thank you," Maggie said. She focused on her purse, which she set down by her feet.

"No, sir," Dwight said.

Boudreaux sat down in his plush leather chair and folded his hands on his desk before he levelled those eyes at Maggie. "What can I do for you today, Maggie?"

"A woman's body was found in Scipio Creek yesterday," she said.

"Yes, I heard."

"That woman had your phone number written down," Maggie said. "When I called here yesterday, your secretary said she'd been to see you."

"You're telling me, then, that Ms. Corzo is the woman who was found," Boudreaux said.

"Yes."

"I'm sorry to hear that," Boudreaux said politely. "Yes, she was here, very briefly, the day before yesterday."

"Can I ask how you know her?"

"I don't, really," Boudreaux answered.

His tone was polite, but Maggie felt like their eyes were having a separate conversation. She wasn't interested in participating. "Why was she here, then?" Maggie couldn't help the tightness creeping into her voice. She didn't have the patience at the moment for Boudreaux's policy of waiting to be asked.

"She said she was here on behalf of her boss," Boudreaux said. "That he wanted to know if I was open to a business arrangement. I wasn't."

"What kind of arrangement?"

"Using my trucking business to transport his products north."

"What kinds of products?"

"I don't know, exactly," Boudreaux answered. "She was somewhat coy about that. I seldom appreciate coyness. I assume they were drugs."

"Why?"

"Because she said her employer, who I gathered was also her significant other, was interested in safely expanding his territory beyond Tampa."

"You didn't ask?" Maggie asked him. She didn't bother disguising her doubt.

"I didn't need to," he answered. "It was drugs. As you know very well, I don't have anything to do with drugs."

"Not up to your moral standards, Mr. Boudreaux?" Maggie asked quietly, before knowing she would.

Boudreaux's eyes narrowed just slightly, and he folded his hands on his desk. "Not the applicable ones, no."

"Did she say who the employer-slash-boyfriend was?"

"No. This was an exploratory meeting, I take it," Boudreaux answered. "She seemed pretty proud of the fact that I was her idea."

"Why *were* you her idea?"

"Maggie," Boudreaux said. "Let's not dance around."

Maggie couldn't help the hint of a smile that appeared on her face. "But I love to dance."

Boudreaux glanced over at Dwight, whose fingers slowed their drumming on the arm of his chair, then he looked back at Maggie.

"Yes," he said simply.

"It's genetic, apparently," Maggie said.

"I'm sure it is," he said quietly, and even though she could see the irritation in his eyes, looking into them reminded her of how safe she'd felt slow dancing with him that night. How sad she'd been that she probably wouldn't have that chance again.

She swallowed, and glanced down at his hands. She wasn't in the mood to regret anything, or to miss anything, either.

"How were things left?" she asked.

"They were left at 'no,'" he answered. "I have no interest in drugs, and I don't do business with strangers, especially those that send their girlfriends to introduce them."

"Did you have anything to do with her ending up in Scipio Creek?" she asked him, then regretted it. Even she knew it was a revenge question.

He levelled those bright blue eyes at her. "Don't ask me questions you know the answers to," he said quietly.

She refused to blink or to look away. "Which questions do you mean?" she asked simply.

Boudreaux glanced at Dwight, but just barely. "I'm referring to the conversation at hand," he said.

"Are you upset with me, Mr. Boudreaux?"

"Of course not," he said, and he just managed not to snap at her. "That would be unreasonable, don't you think?"

"What else did Ms. Corzo say during your meeting?" Maggie asked.

He stared at her a moment before answering. "She was here fewer than ten minutes," he said. "She introduced herself as Axel Blackwell's ex-wife, said she knew of me from her brief time here, and thought I might be interested in doing business. People think I'm a lot more diversified than I actually am."

"You are a complex guy," Maggie said.

"Not that complex," he replied shortly.

"Did you refer her to anyone else, since you weren't interested?"

"I don't associate with the type of people she needed to pitch, Maggie," he said calmly. "And I'm not interested in being a matchmaker for people who want to bring more drug trade to the Panhandle. If her boyfriend wants to establish himself here, he'll have to do his own homework."

Maggie knew he was telling her the truth. She knew his position on drugs. She didn't want to be glad for it but she was anyway.

"Do you have any other questions for me, Maggie?"

"Quite a few," she answered. "But they can wait."

She grabbed her purse and stood up, and Dwight seemed slightly startled that the interview was over. He quickly stood as well. Boudreaux was slower about it.

"I don't think they should," he said. He glanced over at Dwight. "Perhaps we could speak privately for a moment?"

Dwight glanced over at Maggie.

"That's not necessary," she said with a polite smile. "We can catch up some other time."

Boudreaux let out a slow breath. "I'll be available when you're ready," he said.

Maggie started for the door, and Dwight beat her to it and opened it for them. Maggie thought he looked like an egret eager to escape a beach full of gulls. She felt badly for making him nervous.

Boudreaux followed them to the door and held it open for Maggie as Dwight walked into the hall.

"It was good to see you, Maggie," he said quietly.

Maggie swallowed and looked away. When she looked directly into those startling blue eyes, it made her angrier, and yet made her want to be less angry. He had hurt her, and yet she felt the temptation to ask him to repair that hurt. The conflict between the two exhausted and incensed her by turns.

Dwight fell in step beside her as they walked back down the carpeted hallway. His Adam's apple bobbed a few times before he spoke.

"It's none of my business, but that was kinda chillier than I was expecting," Dwight said. "You know, on account of y'all are friendly."

"Not today," Maggie said quietly.

"He's pretty scary when he's not."

Maggie just nodded. She needed to calm down. She needed to not talk anymore.

"Tell you what," Dwight said. "Every time the guy looked at me, I felt like someone stuck a Popsicle down the front of my shorts." He glanced over at Maggie. "'Scuse the expression."

They were silent again until they'd stepped out into the November sun. It was noon, and Maggie was momentarily blinded. When she stopped to fish for her sunglasses, Dwight put his hands on his hips.

"Hey, uh, Maggie?" he started, looking somewhere around her throat. "You can tell me it's none of my business, but I know how much Wyatt loves you and all—"

Maggie jerked her glasses out and looked up at Dwight. "I would never do that, Dwight. This wasn't some lover's quarrel," she said quickly. She swallowed hard. "He's my father. And if you ever repeat that, I'll punch you in the throat."

She stalked away toward the Jeep. Dwight stood there a moment, looking after her. "Bless my bony ass," he said under his breath.

CHAPTER TEN

The drive back to Eastpoint was primarily a silent one. Dwight cut his eyes over to Maggie a few times, but he left her alone for the ten minutes it took them to get back to the Sheriff's Office. It wasn't until she'd parked and shut off the Cherokee that Dwight spoke up.

"I would never say anything, Maggie," he said quietly.

Maggie sighed. "I know. I didn't mean to insult you," she said quietly.

"But, geez, Maggie," he said. "How the hell'd you keep *that* a secret for so long?"

"By not knowing," she said. "I'm sorry, but can we not talk about this anymore?"

"Yeah. Yeah, sure," he said, and opened his door.

Maggie got out and they headed for the glass front doors of the low-slung tan building.

"Wyatt knows, though, right?"

"Yes," she answered. "Wyatt knows everything."

"Well, that's what we've always said," he mumbled.

Maggie and Dwight parted ways once they were inside, he to the deputies' office to check with Larry about the autopsy he'd started just after Marisol's family had left, and Maggie to check on the numbers from Marisol's phone.

She walked into the small IT department down the hall from Wyatt's office. Jake Manning was typing on his keyboard, fingers flying, while he watched a video on his iPad.

"Hey, Jake?"

"Hey, Maggie," he answered, looking over his shoulder. "You here for your phone numbers?"

"Yeah."

"One sec," he said. He kept typing, his eyes back on his video. Maggie couldn't tell what it was, but she heard laughter, and Jake smiled to himself. He was one of the younger deputies in the department, somewhere around his late twenties, with a boyish face and a physique that could use a few bowls of stew.

Maggie wandered over to his cluttered desk while she waited. After a moment, he stopped typing, tapped at the iPad screen, and the room went quiet.

"Yeah, so most of this stuff looks pretty uninteresting," he said as he rummaged through a short pile of folders. "Probably girlfriends, that kind of thing. A few stylists, some chick that does bikini waxing, and some other lady that apparently does some kind of detox thing. It scared me to ponder."

He pulled out a brown file folder and opened it up.

"Did you get a chance to pull the file on Toby Mann?" Maggie asked.

"Yeah, he's a sweetheart," Jake answered as he read. "Couple of convictions for possession with intent, coke and meth. Did six months and nine months respectively. Last one was almost four years ago. Apparently, he has several small businesses, and a real nice condo on Bayshore Blvd."

"Okay," Maggie said. "What about this guy Gavin Betancourt? Did you run him down?"

"Oh, yeah. He's kind of a mucky muck over there," Jake said. "Connected, you know? Owns like five houses up and down the Gulf Coast—"

"Does he have one here?" Maggie interrupted.

"No, but give him a minute," Jake said. He looked back down at the file. "One on Cedar Key, two in Tampa, one in Sanibel and a condo down in Key West."

"Wow," Maggie said.

"Yeah. He has a crap-ton of legitimate businesses," Jake said. "Bunch of commercial real estate, some restaurants, a yacht club down in Bimini. Most of his traceable money is from those, but Tampa and the DEA say he's one of the key distributors for coke and heroin down there."

"That's nice," Maggie said.

"Yeah, we like him a lot," Jake said.

"Was his number in her phone?"

"In a roundabout way," Mike answered. "Listed under Bayside Realty Management. Three calls. One on Tuesday, looks long enough to maybe go to voice mail, but not long enough for a conversation. Two more on Wednesday, but they weren't answered." He closed the file. "Anyway, those are the highlights on the contacts. As far as the rest of the numbers from her phone, I made you a list, but it's pretty bare. Like I said, mostly other women and a few businesses."

Maggie took the file from him. "Thanks, Jake," she said.

"At your service, Mags," he said, and was already back to his keyboard and iPad by the time she turned to leave.

She stopped short after just a few steps, and turned back to Jake.

"Hey. Wasn't Toby Mann's number in there?"

Jake looked up from his monitor, but kept typing. "Nope. Why?"

"Well, he's supposed to be her boyfriend. No recent calls, no entry in her contacts list?"

"Neither one," he answered. "But, hey, I don't have my wife in my contacts."

"I bet she's in your recent calls, though," Maggie said.

"Yeah, she's pretty much all of my recent calls."

"Yeah," Maggie said, mainly to herself. "Thanks, Jake."

She walked out into the hall, and headed to her side of the building, slapping the brown file against her thigh. She slowed as she approached Wyatt's office. His door was open, and she spotted him at his desk. He looked up as she leaned on his door jamb.

"Hey," he said.

"Hey," she said tiredly.

"Shut the door and come sit," he said.

"I can't," she answered. "I just ran Dwight back. I've got to get back to town for Axel's bail hearing."

"Anybody in the hall?" he asked.

Maggie looked over her shoulder, then shook her head. "No."

He lowered his voice. "That arrest was crap," he said. "Just because we don't have anybody else to arrest yet doesn't mean we have enough to arrest Axel."

"Well, we do if it looks good on the news," Maggie said.

He looked at her for a moment. "How did it go over at Sea-Fair?"

She sighed. "I wasn't as smooth as I hoped I would be," she said.

"This is a bad time to tell you you're rarely smooth," he said quietly.

"Yeah. Tell me next time." She held up a hand. "I'll see you later."

"See you later," he said.

A few minutes later, she stepped back out into the brightness of the day. When she was halfway across the parking lot, she pulled out her phone and tapped a number from her recent calls list. Wyatt answered on the first ring.

"I love you, though," Maggie said.

"Yeah? Well, that makes up for several of your personality flaws," he said.

Maggie looked over at one of the tall, narrow windows as the blinds opened. Wyatt raised a hand at her.

"Oh, and I love you, too, as it happens," he said. She could hear his smile more clearly than she could see it from that distance.

"Well, then I'm not a total loss," she said.

She hung up, climbed into the Jeep, and headed back to Apalach.

⚓ ⚓ ⚓

Maggie sat behind Axel and his attorney, Howard Fairchild, as Fairchild and the State's Attorney, Bryan Drummond, presented their cases to His Honor Vernon Greer.

Maggie stared at the back of Howard's head. He was a black man in his fifties or early sixties, thin and a couple of inches shorter than Axel's six feet, but when he spoke he reminded Maggie of James Earl Jones. She'd known him for ten years, but she was surprised every time he opened his mouth.

She shook her head a bit and tried to focus on what Drummond was saying.

"Your Honor, it's the state's position that Mr. Blackwell is a flight risk," he was saying. "He has a boat at his disposal, and he could flee across the Gulf to Mexico pretty much at any time."

Howard Fairchild leaned forward over the table and looked at Drummond. "Where the hell are you *from*, Drummond?"

"Mr. Fairchild," Judge Greer said quietly.

"Apologies, Your Honor," Fairchild said politely. "Where the hell are you from, *Mr.* Drummond?"

The judge sighed, and Drummond puffed his chest out a bit, what there was of it behind his hundred-dollar shirt. "Gainesville," he answered, as though this was something to be proud of.

"Oh, well that explains it," Fairchild answered. "Not a lot of boats in Gainesville."

"What bearing does that have?" Drummond asked.

"Mr. Blackwell is a shrimper, Mr. Drummond," Fairchild answered. "He owns a *trawler*. You could ride your bicycle to Mexico and be there in time to catch his stern line for him." He looked at the judge. "Your Honor, Mr. Blackwell was born and raised in this community. Aside from a high school trip to DC, he's never even been out of the state. He has two children here in Franklin County. He's committed to his life here, and to clearing his name. Ms. Corzo may have been his ex-wife, but she was still a friend. He's committed to assisting law enforcement in any way possible to find and prosecute whoever is responsible for taking her life in this terrible manner."

The judge wet the dentures beneath his white moustache before speaking. "I see no reason to expect Mr. Blackwell to abscond, Mr. Drummond. I also see very little evidence thus far in the case against him. I feel your charges are preemptive at best. Bail is set at $25,000. "

"Thank you, Your Honor," Fairchild answered.

"Mr. Blackwell, the bailiff will escort you to pay your bond and then you're free to go," the judge said. Axel nodded. "Mr. Fairchild, please advise your client of his responsibilities."

"Yes, Your Honor," Fairchild said politely.

The judge turned to the bailiff, a slim woman in her fifties with dyed red hair and cat-eye glasses. "Edith, be a dear and get me some sweet tea before you call the next case."

He tapped his gavel against the desk. "Five minute recess, everyone."

Maggie stood when Fairchild and Axel did. Drummond started stuffing paperwork into an expensive attaché case. He looked over at Fairchild with a smirk.

"I certainly hope this won't be a trend, divorce lawyers in criminal court," he said.

Fairchild snapped his own weathered case shut and picked it up. "It likely will be if divorce lawyers keep kicking your ass," he said.

Drummond stalked up the aisle toward the door as a young, male bailiff came and stood beside the defense table.

"Go pay up, Axel," Fairchild said.

"I'll meet you out front," Maggie said. "Then I'll run you back to your truck."

"Okay," Axel said. "Thanks, Howard."

The men shook hands. "My pleasure, mostly," Fairchild said.

They watched Axel walk out the side door, then Fairchild looked at Maggie. "I hope you come up with a better suspect, because a bail hearing is one thing, but he doesn't need to depend on me in a murder trial. Not even against that dumbass."

CHAPTER
ELEVEN

Maggie and Axel stopped at the Apalachicola Coffee Company on Market Street. While Maggie went inside to get the coffees, leaving Axel to Axel plug his cell into her charger and call his kids.

Apalachicola Coffee was cool without trying hard. Exposed brick walls, high ceilings, burlap coffee sacks hanging on the walls. Maggie's favorite thing, aside from the coffee, was the smell of the coffee. Every time she walked in, she felt a peace seep into her soul. She was an addict, but like most addicts, she was unapologetic about it.

She walked up to the espresso counter at the back, bracing herself for the usual hard time from the owner, George, but it was a young guy with a short ponytail who stepped out from the kitchen. Maggie didn't know him.

"What can I get ya?" he asked.

Maggie was a little taken aback. George hadn't hired anyone new in years. "Where's George?" she asked.

"Sold the place," the guy answered, looking fairly unenthusiastic about conversation that didn't include an order. "I'm Kirk, the new owner."

Maggie swallowed and tried to regroup. She hadn't been in the shop in almost a month. Money had been tight. But it was only a month. "Sold it? Why?" She tried not to sound stricken. She didn't like change all that much. Or at all.

"Job stress," Kirk answered flatly. "You know, customers. Don't worry; same beans, better coffee." He placed a hand on a gleaming, antique-looking espresso machine that was bigger than Maggie. "New machine. Very sexy."

"Well," Maggie said. "Crap."

He glanced at the emblem on her polo shirt. "So, you must be the one from the Sheriff's Office."

"Yeah," Maggie answered. "What do you mean?"

"George left me nine pages of barely legible notes. You were on four of them," he said.

"What kind of notes?"

"Barely legible ones," he answered, his eyelids at half-mast. "For instance, he said to tell you you don't need an extra shot in your coffee, since we already put two shots in and they're not thimble-sized shots of that crap from Starbucks. He also said you wouldn't actually shoot me, but I would have figured that out on my own."

Maggie's eyes narrowed. "And why is that?"

"Because I haven't made your coffee yet, and you don't know how to operate the sexy machine." He grabbed a small stainless carafe and placed it on the counter. "One coffee or two?"

"Three," she answered.

"Why?"

Maggie could feel her fingers twitching. "One of them is for someone else," she said.

He looked over her shoulder, out the plate glass window. "Him?"

Maggie looked over her shoulder. Axel was sitting in the driver's seat of the Jeep, talking on the phone. She looked back at Kirk, the apparent guardian of the caffeine galaxy. "Yeah," she said.

"One with an extra shot, kid temperature, no cardboard, for now," he said flatly. "One regular temperature, with cardboard, for later. What about his?"

Maggie's eyes narrowed again. "Regular temperature, regular shots, regular cardboard," she answered.

⚓ ⚓ ⚓

A few minutes later, a young couple held the door for Maggie as she left the shop carrying the three cups. Axel was leaning against the Jeep, and met her on the sidewalk.

"Which one's mine?" he asked.

"This one," she answered, pointing with her chin.

He took one of the cups from her. "Are you drinking both of those?"

"Yes," she said, a little defensively. She thought about asking him if he knew George had sold the place, but Axel drank Maxwell House from a beige Mr. Coffee. She opened her door and set her extra cup in the cup holder, then stood by Axel and took a sip of her coffee as he fired up a cigarette. He inhaled deeply, then blew out a thick plume of smoke.

"Thanks, Maggie," he said.

"For what?"

He shrugged and shook his head. "The coffee."

"Did you talk to the kids?" Maggie asked him.

He nodded and took another drag of his cigarette. "You remember the time we camped out on the bay?"

Maggie smiled. "Yeah."

The three of them had been sixteen. They'd taken Axel's father's old Chris Craft and anchored off of Dog Island for the weekend. It had been October, and the weather had been cool and clear. They'd eaten Fig Newtons and cold Spaghetti-Os and slept on a pallet on deck. Maggie slept in the middle because Axel thought sleeping next to David would impinge on his manliness. He'd always needed a seat between them at the movies, too.

"I couldn't sleep that first night, and I sat up smoking for a while," Axel said, staring off at the street or the distant past. "I remember watching you and David, and thinking you'd probably have four kids by the time you were thirty, and I'd probably never even get married."

Maggie felt a dull pain somewhere in her chest. "Well, nobody ever said you were psychic," she said.

He gave her half a smile. "Nope. I can't stop getting married, and I have just as many kids as you do."

"They're good kids, Axel."

He glanced at her as he exhaled another cloud of smoke, twisting his mouth to point it away from her. "Yeah, I can't imagine how that happened."

"Don't give me that crap, Axel. You might try to come off as a complete jerk, but you're a good guy."

Axel looked over at her, and his eyes seemed to have lost some of their color, like the bay will when the cloud cover is low and heavy.

"I love you, Maggie," he said quietly. "But we both know there isn't one thing I do right on land."

⚓ ⚓ ⚓

Axel's truck was right where he'd left it, parked two spots down from Maggie's usual space. She pulled in, then walked with him to his truck. She leaned up against the side as he unlocked his door.

"Axel, can you think of anything else Marisol told you about her boyfriend?" she asked.

"The only times Mari ever talked much about her guys was when she felt like rubbing it in," he said. "This wasn't one of those times. She just wanted to get together, spend time."

"Did she say his name?"

Axel thought a minute, staring over the roof of his truck at the overgrown acreage behind the Sheriff's Office and county jail. "No, I don't think so."

"Did she mention the name Toby?"

Axel shook his head slowly. "No." He looked at her. "She did say something about him being a classy guy, but we didn't talk too much about our lives this time around. She seemed like maybe she just wanted to relax a little, get away from things."

"Was she tense? Scared?"

Axel pulled his pack of cigarettes out of his shirt pocket, slid a cigarette out, and lit it. Then he squinted into his first exhalation before speaking. "Mari never felt one way at a time," he said. "She was trying hard to have fun." He looked over at her. "It seemed like maybe she was trying too hard, you know what I mean?"

"Yeah, maybe," Maggie said. Over Axel's shoulder, she saw Wyatt walking toward them across the parking lot. She looked back at Axel. "You want to come over and have some dinner or something?"

He shook his head. "No. Thanks. I'm gonna run over to Carrabelle, stop by and see the kids for a minute."

"Hey, Axel," Wyatt said as he approached.

"Hey, man," Axel said. "How's it going?"

Wyatt shook Axel's hand. "Okay. How are you doing?"

Axel gave him something between a nod and a shrug.

"I'm sorry about your ex-wife," Wyatt said quietly.

"Thanks." Axel swung himself into the driver's seat of his truck. "I'm heading out." He looked at Maggie. "I'll call you tomorrow, see how it's going, okay?"

She nodded at him. "Okay."

She and Wyatt watched him drive off, then Wyatt frowned down at her. "So, your dad called me. Twice," he said.

Maggie sighed. "Okay. And?"

"You need to go talk to him," Wyatt answered. "He said if you don't, he's coming by the house."

"I don't want to talk to him about this with the kids around," she said, irritated.

"I think that's the point," Wyatt said.

Maggie chewed at the corner of her lip. "We're supposed to have dinner, remember?"

"I have to cancel," Wyatt said as he turned to walk away.

"Why?" Maggie asked his back.

"Because he said so," Wyatt said. He lifted a hand, though he didn't look back. "Come by after, if you feel like it."

⚓ ⚓ ⚓

Maggie's parents lived on Hwy 98, just outside the city limits. The area was a mixture of commercial and residential property and was certainly nothing fancy, but it had been affordable bayfront property back when Maggie was a kid; affordable enough that her folks had recently paid off their mortgage.

Maggie pulled onto the property and slowly drove down the long, oyster shell driveway that led to the house, a neat, clapboard cottage that was painted a soft gray and featured a wide porch in front and a brand new deck in back. As the drive curved around a tall palm, Maggie could just see that her father was sitting on the dock out back.

The house was in the middle of the two-acre parcel, which made it far enough back from the busy road, but also gave her parents a large back yard that ended at their weathered dock. Maggie parked out front next to her dad's old pickup. Her mother's car was in the open garage.

Maggie had been loved here, and she tried to remember that, as she listened to her engine ticking.

Finally, she got out of the Cherokee and headed around the house. There was a good, dry breeze, calmed just a bit with the setting sun, and the water out on the bay was just slightly choppy. The breeze carried the smells of brine and silt and sea grasses to Maggie, and she closed her eyes a moment to allow them to calm her.

Gray was sitting at the end of the dock, his long legs hanging over the edge. He had a Stella Artois sitting beside him. It was half full. His old oyster skiff bumped gently against its fenders beside him, the color of its chipped and peeling turquoise paint just a bit deeper in the twilight.

As Maggie walked through the back yard, she watched the sun set Daddy's sandy hair to sparkling, saw the breeze shove it over his eyes, watched him reach up to shove it back. Her father was a few inches shorter than Wyatt and about fifty pounds lighter but, as lanky as he was, decades of hard work had made him strong and fit.

When Maggie's hiking boots clomped onto the wooden planks, Gray looked over his shoulder at her, then looked back out to the bay. Maggie stopped just behind him.

"I'm still not ready to talk to you about this, Daddy," she said.

Gray sighed out at the bay. "Well, Margaret Anne, get yourself good and ready, because now is when we're going to talk about it."

Maggie stood there a moment, her hands curled into fists in the pockets of her sweater.

"Sit down, Sunshine," Daddy said quietly.

Maggie sat down beside him. Her legs hung over the side, her feet only reaching halfway down her daddy's legs.

They were silent for some time, both of them looking out at the water that had always given them solace and a solid footing.

"That was a wild thing you did, with Boudreaux," Gray said.

Maggie glanced over at her father's profile, then back out at the bay. "I didn't know what else to do," she said. "Nobody was talking."

"We've been talking about talking about it," Gray said. "For some time."

Maggie felt the anger curling up from somewhere around her gut, and she kept her mouth shut. Gray didn't look at her when he spoke again.

"I think you scared him pretty good," he said.

"He had that coming," Maggie said tightly. "He had no business starting some kind of friendship with me, without me knowing."

Gray looked over at her finally. The sun-carved lines around his mouth seemed deeper than they had just a month ago. "We agreed a long time ago, the three of us, that he would have no part in your life," he said. "He kept to that agreement, until you started working his nephew's suicide. You know it bothered me a great deal, when you two started talking, spending time together, but it wasn't really in my hands."

"He should have just told me," she said.

"Apparently that was his intention, back in the summer," Gray said.

"Let me guess. Mom didn't want to," Maggie said, and wasn't especially successful at keeping the bitterness out of her tone.

Gray looked over at her. He had that look he'd always gotten when she'd overstepped herself as a teenager. "Actually, Maggie, it was me that wasn't ready."

Maggie swallowed and stared at her father. He looked back out at the bay.

"One of the great joys of my life has been that you are such a daddy's girl," he said quietly. "To some extent, I suppose I encouraged it as a way to get back at your mama a little, even though I forgave her long before you were born." He looked over at her. "She took it gracefully, I think. I could see that it hurt her sometimes, the way you'd spend all your time with me. But it didn't bother me enough to change it. She took it as her due, I think."

"All my life, Daddy, I have held you guys up as my ideal, the perfect marriage, the marriage I wanted," she said.

He looked over at her. "You'd be fortunate indeed, Sunshine," he said. "I love her more than I did last month or ten years ago, more than when we were teenagers."

"How?"

"Maggie, do you realize that we were only a couple of years older than Sky at that time? Do you understand when Sky makes a mistake born of immaturity?"

"Daddy, she cheated on you," Maggie said.

"Listen to me. It was one night. One time. The night Holden Crawford went missing."

Maggie swallowed hard. "Mom was Boudreaux's alibi for that night," she said.

"Yes. She told your grandfather, and he told Sheriff Wilson," her father answered. "A few days later, Boudreaux went back to Louisiana and we didn't hear anything about him again, or see him, until a he came back a few months later. Of course, by then we knew your mama was expecting, and for reasons I don't care to discuss, we knew you were his."

Maggie stared at his profile for a moment. His jaw tightened and released just perceptibly. "She lost her virginity with Boudreaux?" she asked tightly.

"That's not going to be part of our conversation, girl," he said quietly. He sighed and took a drink of his beer, then looked back at her. "We did what we thought was best for everybody, especially you. We made the best decision we could at the time."

"I wish you had told me this when I started getting to know him," Maggie said.

"I wish I had, too. Maggie, you know I don't think that much of Boudreaux," Gray said. "And I didn't want you to get involved with him. But, he kept his word. He stayed out of your life and out of our way. I respect him for that."

Maggie opened her mouth to say something smart, then changed her mind. She looked out at the water and wished she was on it.

"I also think he's come to genuinely care for you," her father added. "And I respect him for that, too."

Maggie swallowed hard, stared out at the water, and wished she could stop the one tear from coursing down her cheek. She blinked a few times to prevent it, but it fled anyway. Out of the corner of her eye, she saw her father staring at her.

"You care for him," he said simply.

Maggie didn't have an answer that she actually wanted to give him, so she said nothing.

"I don't think being with him can be good for you, even if you weren't a police officer. But it's your right, Maggie," he said, then sighed. "I suppose it's his right, too."

They were silent for a moment. Maggie resisted the urge to drop her head onto her father's shoulder.

"Daddy, I don't even know who to be," she said finally.

Gray looked down at her, his eyes kind, but pained. "Maggie, none of this changes who we are…who you are."

"But that's not true, really, is it?" Maggie asked. "Every single day, I realize something else. I don't live in my grandfather's house, I just live in the house your father built. I'm not—we've gone to the Highlands Festival every year since I can remember, and I can even speak a little Scots Gaelic, but I'm not Scottish! I don't even know what I am!"

"You're my daughter," Gray said quietly. "Our daughter. And your grandparents are still your grandparents."

"Daddy, I have one bloodline that isn't even mine, and another one that I know nothing about," Maggie said wearily.

Gray nodded. "I know. And I don't know anything about all that," he said. "You'll have to talk to him about that."

Maggie felt the heat of anger and humiliation and resentment in the center of her being.

"I don't want to talk to him about it," she said.

"I expect you will, eventually," he said.

Maggie chewed at the corner of her lip, working hard at not saying anything flip. "I need to go, Daddy." She stood up, and Gray stood with her.

He pulled her to him and she let him, but she had to step back more quickly than she normally would. She despised losing control of her emotions, and there were few things that made her more emotional than her father's embrace.

Gray frowned down at her. "Maggie, I'm sorry. I didn't want you to figure it out; I wanted to be man enough to tell you myself. I just wasn't."

Maggie nodded, but she couldn't think of one thing to say.

"Bye, Daddy," she said, and turned to go. "I'm going to stop inside and use the bathroom."

"Maggie? There's only one person on this earth that I love as much as I do you," Gray said gently. "If you go in that house, you need to mind how you speak to my wife. Do you understand?"

Maggie looked at him a moment, then nodded and walked away. She stopped about ten feet shy of the deck steps, and looked at the house. Then she changed direction and headed for the driveway. She would use her own bathroom.

CHAPTER TWELVE

The next morning, Maggie was at her desk, calling the people on Marisol's contacts list, when Dwight stuck his head through her door.

"Hey, Maggie? Uh, that guy Toby Mann is here to see you."

Maggie stared at him a moment, then disconnected the call she hadn't finished dialing. "Here?"

"Yeah," Dwight answered. "He just walked in here and said he wanted to talk to you. Said he saw the thing on the news."

"Well then," she said, mostly to herself.

"Yeah. You want me to bring him back here?"

"No, take him to one of the interview rooms," Maggie answered. "I'll be right there."

"Okeedoke," he said. "When we're done with him, I've got Larry's report on Marisol's autopsy."

"Was she strangled?"

"Yeah."

"Anything else interesting?" she asked.

"Maybe a couple things, yeah," he said.

"Okay, I'll be right there," Maggie said.

Dwight disappeared from her doorway, and Maggie fished around in her desk drawer for a fresh pen. She couldn't handle ball points, which was all the office bought, and preferred to bring in her own roller balls. She found one, then grabbed her planner-size notebook and her coffee and headed out.

Mann was sitting in Room 2. Maggie took a moment to look at him through the small window in the door as he talked to Dwight. He was slim, maybe about thirty-five, with stylishly cut dark brown hair. Though he was seated, Maggie figured he was about five ten or eleven. He was handsome, though a little too South Beach for her taste.

She opened the door, and Dwight stopped in the middle of whatever he was saying. Mann stood up when she entered. She closed the door quietly, then walked over to the table.

"Mr. Mann? I'm Lt. Redmond," she said. She was glad her hands were full, which kept him from holding out a hand, should he be so inclined.

"Yes," he said. His voice, like the one on his voice mail message, was smooth, though not especially deep. "I'm sorry I didn't return your calls. I just found out yesterday, and I've been kind of out of it."

Maggie nodded and they both sat down. Dwight took the seat next to Maggie.

"Marisol was your girlfriend?" Maggie asked.

He nodded, swallowing. "Yes. For the last few months, although we were acquaintances for a while before that."

"How did you meet?"

"At a party, for a mutual friend," he said. "Last spring."

Maggie jotted that down. "She worked with you as well?"

"She helped me out here and there," he said. "Helped plan dinners and parties and things for business associates, helped me with PR and stuff."

"What kind of PR?"

He shrugged slightly. "I own some food trucks that do very well, a couple of small restaurants. Marisol helped with advertising, getting us in the paper, getting reviews, that sort of thing." He coughed into his hand. Maggie couldn't tell if he was choking up or just had a dry throat. "She was good at it, good with people. She was good for business."

"How about your other business?" Maggie asked. "Was she good for that, too?"

He looked at her, his slightly hooded eyes expressionless. "I don't have any other businesses," he said quietly.

"You have two convictions for selling narcotics," she replied.

"That was then, this is now," he answered calmly. "There are easier ways to make money. Ways that don't get you thrown in jail."

"So you're out of that line of work?"

"Yes, I am," he said. "You probably don't believe that, but there's nothing I can do about that."

"I don't really have a reason not to believe it," Maggie said, which wasn't actually true. Boudreaux didn't lie to her much, at least not about anything related to her work. And Tampa PD didn't seem to think Toby Mann had retired. "Where were you Wednesday night and Thursday?"

"Home. In Tampa, I mean," he said.

"Can anybody verify that for us?"

"Well, I mean, I saw friends," he said. "I did have a grand re-opening, too. On Wednesday evening. There were newspapers there. I was in the paper."

"Okay," Maggie said. "Can I ask why you're here?"

"Well, to talk to you," he answered.

"It's a five hour drive up from Tampa," Maggie said. "Why didn't you just return my calls?"

He looked at her for a moment and swallowed before answering. "I don't mean any disrespect, but I thought maybe you'd work a little harder at putting away the person who did this if someone was here. You know, somebody that knew her."

"Her ex-husband lives here," she said. "Were you aware of that?"

"Yeah, she told me about him a long time ago," he said. "I also know you arrested him for killing her."

"The charge was suspicion of murder, Mr. Mann," she said. "That's all it is at this point."

"Look, I'm not from a small town, but I know how things tend to work, okay?" he said. "He's a local guy. You're local people. I'm not saying he'd automatically get a pass. I just want things to be done right for Marisol."

"Do you have some reason to think her ex-husband would have hurt her, Mr. Mann?" Maggie asked.

He shrugged. "Well, I mean, he's her ex. They have a weird history, back and forth sometimes, you know? Marisol said he was still hung up on her."

"Did you know she was coming here?"

"No. Not until I heard what happened."

"And how did you hear about that?"

"It was on the news, online," he said. "I saw it Thursday night, after I got back from the grand opening."

"Yet you didn't return my calls on Friday," she said.

"Look, I was upset," he said. "I also knew you'd probably look at me, because we were together, and because of my history. Which is just that: history."

Maggie didn't buy that he was unaware Marisol was in Apalach. She'd told Axel and Boudreaux both that she was here on behalf of her boyfriend.

"Does it bother you that she was here?" she asked, watching his eyes.

He shrugged again. She was tired of him shrugging. "Because her ex is here? Look, I don't want to look like an ass or anything, but she and I weren't that invested in each other, you know what I mean?"

"No."

Toby looked at Dwight, then back at Maggie. "Probably easier for a guy to understand. I mean, Marisol was a beautiful woman. We had a good time together, we worked well together. But I wasn't in love with her or anything. It's not like we were thinking of getting married, you know?"

"So it was a casual relationship," Maggie said.

"Well, yeah. More or less."

"And yet you drove all the way up here to make sure she gets some justice," Maggie said flatly.

"Yeah. I'm not saying I didn't care about her," he said. "She deserved better than what she got."

Maggie chewed at the corner of her lip for a moment. "What about her previous boyfriend, Gavin Betancourt? What do you know about him?"

"That jerk," Troy said, his lip curling. "Another example of her deserving better."

"How's that?"

"He treated her like crap," Troy answered. "Rich guy, thinks he can do what he wants. She left him for me. He slapped her around."

"I see," Maggie said.

Dwight looked over at Maggie. "Hey, uh, can I talk to you a second outside?"

"Yeah," she answered, standing. "We'll be back in just a minute, Mr. Mann."

"Yeah, sure," he said.

Dwight followed Maggie out into the hall. They moved down from the door a few feet, and Maggie turned to face him. "What's up?"

"Well, the autopsy," Dwight said. "Larry says she had some injuries, you know, older ones, not from the other night."

"Like what?"

"One was a fractured wrist. Didn't look like it had been set," Dwight answered. "Near as he could say, it was a few months old."

Maggie nodded. "Okay. What do you think about this guy?"

"I think he's slick," Dwight answered. "I can't stand slick."

"You think anything he's saying is true?"

"I doubt he tells the truth much, but this thing about Betancourt beating her, that might be true, huh?"

"Maybe," Maggie answered. "Did you have any luck tracking him down this morning?"

"No, his secretary said he's still out on some boat trip," Dwight answered. "She's real polite and all, but I can kindly drop dead while I wait for him to get back to me at his convenience."

"Okay," Maggie said. "Why don't you ask him a few questions when we go back in?"

"Me?"

"Yeah, you," she answered. "Training."

"I think you asked him everything I would ask," he said.

Maggie started back toward the room. "Well, think up something else," she said, as Dwight followed. "Ask him where he gets his hair cut."

"Girly World, most likely," Dwight mumbled.

She opened the door, and Toby looked up as she and Dwight took their seats again.

"Uh, Mr. Mann?" Dwight started. Toby looked at him, looking surprised that Dwight was actually addressing him. "How long did you say you and Ms. Corzo knew each other?"

"Well, we met back in the spring," he said. "But we got together a few months ago. Late August, early September?"

"And she left Mr. Betancourt for you?"

"Yes."

"Why? Because he hit her?"

"Yeah. Plus he just treated her like crap," Tobu answered.

"How did he feel about her leaving him?"

Toby hesitated before answering. "Look, he's a pretty powerful guy, okay? I'm not looking to get nailed because I said he might have wanted to kill her or something."

"But abusers are kinda territorial, right? They get pretty upset when the women they're abusing leave 'em," Dwight answered. "Did he come after her, try to get her back?"

"Not that I know about," Toby answered. "I would have done something about that."

Dwight nodded noncommittally and looked over at Maggie. "I can't think of anything else right this minute," he said.

Mann sat up straighter in his chair, looking like he'd be happy to be done. "When can I get Mari's things?"

"Any effects that weren't needed for the investigation have been turned over to Marisol's family," Maggie said.

Mann looked uncomfortable, and at the same time like he was trying hard not to look uncomfortable. "Well, okay, that's cool," he said. "As long as everything's taken care of."

Maggie chewed her lip a moment. "Did Marisol have a cell phone, Mr. Mann?"

He seemed surprised by the question. "Well, yeah. You don't have it?"

"What kind of phone is it?" Maggie asked, ignoring the question.

He pulled a black iPhone 6 out of his blazer pocket. "I got her one just like mine," he said, and Maggie sensed he was proud of that. "Put her on my plan, because her credit was crap. I tried to help her out, you know? I even put her on one of my credit cards, for the business."

Maggie nodded thoughtfully, wrote that down. "How long will you be in town, Mr. Mann?" she asked.

"A few days, at least," he said. "I'd appreciate it if you could keep me updated, you know? I'm staying at the Water Street Hotel."

"Which room?"

"I don't know, I haven't checked in yet," he answered. "But you can get me on my cell, 24/7." He managed to look apologetic. "I'll answer this time."

Maggie stood up, Dwight quickly following suit. Maggie held her hand out to Mann.

"I think that's all for now, Mr. Mann," she said.

He stood up, gave her hand a quick shake. "Okay."

A few minutes later, Maggie and Dwight watched through the break room window as Mann walked to a dark blue car, got in and drove away.

"What kind of car is that, Dwight?"

"Hyundai," he answered right away. "Elantra." He leaned closer to the window, craned his neck to watch Toby pull out of the parking lot. "South Carolina plates," he said. "Think it's a rental?"

"Why would he rent a car just to drive from Tampa?" Maggie asked. "His DMV says he owns a 2014 BMW."

"Kinda odd," Dwight mused. "Car in the shop, maybe?"

"Too neat," Maggie said quietly. "Do me a favor, and check on the restaurant thing, the grand opening or whatever."

"Okay," he said. "What's the deal with her phone?" Dwight asked.

"Toby Mann wasn't in Marisol's contact list or recent calls," she answered. "Don't you find that odd?"

"I do," he said. "But the phone we found in her room's a Galaxy."

"Exactly. So why does she have two phones, and where's the other one?"

"Reckon we need it," he said. "Reckon he thinks maybe he does, too."

"Maybe. Unless he already has it," she said quietly. "I also didn't see a credit card in her wallet, other than her secured card."

"What are you thinking about that?"

"I think she didn't want to use his phone or his card while she was here," Maggie said.

"If she was here trying to work him a deal, why wouldn't she want him to know she was here?" Dwight asked. "You think maybe on account of Axel?"

"Maybe," Maggie said. "But even so, she's trying to set something up for him with Boudreaux, so he knows she's here, right? And he said he knew Axel lives here."

"Kinda hinky."

"Yeah," Maggie said.

"All right, well, I'll go see about the grand opening thing, then maybe try to find out about the rental car. Anything else?"

"Check back with me after," she said, distracted. "I see Mike's car out front, so I'm headed over to tech to see what he got from the scene."

"Okeedoke," Dwight answered, and they each went their own way in the hall.

⚓ ⚓ ⚓

Maggie opened the door to the small, two room crime tech lab. Mike was at a counter in the front room, making notes in a brown folder. He looked up and smiled as Maggie came in and shut the door.

"Hey, Maggie," he said.

"Hey, Mike," she answered. "What are you doing here on a Saturday?"

"Ah, I'm behind. Thought I'd catch up a little," he said. "You here about Corzo?"

"Yeah, anything good?"

"Not really," he said. He reached underneath the counter and pulled out a deep wide drawer, lifted out a clear box, and set it on the counter. Inside were several pieces of evidence in labelled clear bags.

Maggie stepped over to the counter as he started going through the bags.

"Got a pair of her panties, no semen or anything on them, but that's not really a biggie, since we recovered that from her body," he said.

"Axel?"

"Yeah, but we already knew that, right?" He held up another bag. "Ton of cigarette butts from a soda can on the nightstand. I guess that whole non-smoking thing was a wash. Marlboros with Axel's saliva, Newports with hers. Here's one thing, though," he said. He flipped through the bags and pulled out another. "Lots more Newports. Recovered them down on the dock, over on the Boss end of the hotel."

"How many?" Maggie asked. It looked like a lot.

"Eight," he answered. "All fresh, so I'm thinking they're from that night. I haven't tested these ones for saliva yet, but I'm betting they'll match the ones from the room. They're all smoked down to the nub."

"If she was comfortable smoking up in the room, why was she outside smoking?" The question was more to herself.

"Got me."

"Any Marlboros out there?"

"Nope." He held up another bag. "Found some credit card receipts in the bathroom trash can, and a handful of those wipes you ladies use to take off your makeup."

Maggie didn't, but she didn't correct him. "Do you have your pictures from the scene?"

"Yep, right here." He pulled the folder over. Inside was a manila file folder. "Took quite a few, both outside and in the room."

"Can you sign this out for me?" Maggie asked. "I'm gonna work on it at home later. I need to spend some time with my kids."

"You got it," he answered.

Maggie signed the case file out, then walked back to her office. She grabbed her purse and phone, then stopped and put down the file, looked up a number, and dialed. It was answered on the first ring.

"Thank you for calling the Water Street Hotel & Marina, this is Peggy. May I help you?"

"Hi, Peggy, this is Maggie Redmond," Maggie said.

"Oh, hey. How are you?"

"I'm fine, thanks," Maggie answered. "Can you tell me if you have a guest by the name of Toby Mann registered?"

"Oh, is this a police thing?"

"Just following up on something," Maggie said.

"Ok, one sec," the woman answered. "Yes, we do."

"When did he check in?" Maggie asked.

"Well, check-in's not until three, but he's reserved starting today," Peggy said.

"Did he say how long he was staying?"

"It says three days," Peggy answered.

"Okay, thanks," Maggie said. "What room are you putting him in?"

"Three-twelve. Overlooking the marina."

Maggie thanked the woman and disconnected, then headed out of the office.

CHAPTER
THIRTEEN

Maggie was slicing mushrooms for their salad when she heard the screen door scrape shut. A moment later, one of Wyatt's arms slipped around her waist.

"I thought you were playing corn hole with the kids," she said.

"I was, until I tripped over Stoopid for the seventeenth time," Wyatt answered. "Besides, while the kids are occupied, I wanted to see hear how it went at your Dad's yesterday."

Maggie swallowed, slid a handful of mushrooms into the salad bowl. "As well as can be expected, I guess," she said.

He waited. Maggie had always admired that about him, the patience he had for someone else to figure out what they wanted to say.

"I guess I just assumed that Boudreaux and my mother had some kind of affair," she said. "But it was just a one-night stand."

Wyatt was quiet for a moment. "Okay, so that is kind of surprising," he finally said.

"She was Boudreaux's alibi when Holden Crawford turned up missing," she said quietly.

Wyatt drummed his fingers on her stomach for a moment before answering. "Not Gray."

"No," Maggie answered. "She was losing her virginity with Boudreaux when Crawford got killed."

"Okay," Wyatt said. "But does that make it better or worse?"

Maggie thought about that, although she'd thought about it a lot already. "I guess it makes it better, if anything. The idea of them having a relationship really bothered me."

They were quiet again. Except for the sound of her knife blade gliding softly along the cutting board, the kitchen was silent.

"Try not to take this the wrong way," she said.

"See, I never like anything you say after that," he said.

"I know. It's just…I'm angry with her for cheating on my father, and I'm angry that they lied to me for so long." Maggie stalled for a moment by dumping the rest of the mushrooms into the salad and starting in on a red pepper. "But I have to admit that I'm a little jealous, too."

Wyatt took a moment to answer. "Of her?"

"Yeah," Maggie said quietly.

"I could do with a little explanation," he said.

"It's not that I had any romantic feelings toward him," she said quickly. "I mean, I'm sure I had a little bit of a crush. Why wouldn't I? You said that yourself."

"Yeah," he said cautiously.

"It's just that, I had this thing, this thing that wasn't about being a mom or a cop or a girlfriend. It was something that was just me and him…this friendship, and I have to admit I was flattered that we had it. He doesn't really like people."

"Evidently," he said, and Maggie knew he was trying to lighten things up a little, for both of them. But nothing really wanted to be lightened up.

"But then I find out that he's not spending time with me because of me, he's spending time with me because of who I am, because of *what* I am. And that my mother had some kind of relationship with him long before I met him."

"Okay," Wyatt said.

Maggie dumped the chunks of red pepper into the bowl, then wiped her hands on a dishcloth and turned around. "That sounds bad. I'm not sure I'm explaining it right."

Wyatt frowned down at her, then put both hands on her shoulders. "Look. I'm not going to pretend to understand everything you think or feel about this situation, and I'm not going to pretend to like everything that I *do* understand. But here are a couple of things that *I* think. I think that you're going to have some kind of relationship with Boudreaux regardless, and you're going to have to figure out what that relationship is. Nobody can do that for you."

Maggie nodded at his chest, and Wyatt tucked a finger under her chin and tilted her head back.

"I also think that this thing can either bring you and your mom closer together or not, but that's not circumstances; it's a choice you're going to make."

Maggie could feel some defensiveness wanting to assert itself. Wyatt saw it on her face.

"You always said your mother was too perfect for you to relate to. Well now she's not," he said simply. "She made a mistake when she was just a kid."

"Wyatt—"

"Hold up," he said quietly. "She made that mistake with someone that you considered your friend. I think that's what's really sticking to you. It was Boudreaux. If it had been some other guy, would it be as big a deal as it is right now?"

Maggie opened her mouth to argue his point, but shut it again without answering. She didn't really know the answer for certain, but she knew there was a decent chance that Wyatt was right. Wyatt kissed her on the forehead and then walked over to the fridge.

"Think about this, too," he said, as he grabbed a beer from the fridge. "She was eighteen. The homecoming queen, daughter of the Chief of Police, engaged to the salt of the earth and all that. She could have had an abortion. Instead she just lied." He twisted the cap off the beer and took a pull. "But not to your dad."

Maggie stared at the floor, at a point halfway between them.

"Hey," Wyatt said. She looked up as he took another drink. "I'll support you, whatever you decide," he said as he walked out of the kitchen to the living room. "As long as you decide to do what I tell you."

Maggie stood there for a moment, watching him go, and heard him go back out the screen door. Then she turned to the sink, grabbed the colander full of spaghetti, and took a few pieces out before dumping the pasta into a slowly simmering pot of homemade vodka sauce.

She grabbed a small plastic bowl from the cupboard, dumped the handful of plain noodles into it, and walked out to the front deck.

Her seventeen-year old daughter Sky was tossing her bean bags at the corn hole board in the front yard, while her eleven-year old son Kyle watched. Every time a bean bag dropped through a hole, Stoopid ran over like a border guard on night watch and pecked at the bag.

"You guys, dinner's ready," Maggie called down.

"Can I take my turn?" Kyle called up. "It's the last round."

"Go ahead," Maggie answered, then raised her voice. "Stoopid!"

She tapped at the side of the bowl and Stoopid dashed across the yard and started running up the stairs, wings akimbo, with all the grace of a camel in high heels. She put the bowl down on the deck, and he one-eyed it a second while he warbled sweet nothings at it. Stoopid found spaghetti endlessly fascinating, and they'd probably be able to eat out on the deck in peace.

Maggie turned and walked around to the side deck. Wyatt was sitting at the round table, beer in hand, staring out at the woods, and his profile broke her heart. The laugh lines at the corner of his eye, the dimples at parade rest in his cheek, the long brown lashes as they floated down and then up again. This was her man, and she was more grateful for that fact than for just about anything she could think of.

She took a deep breath, let it out slowly, and then put her hands on her hips, her fingers twisting nervously into her palms.

"So, I'm ready," she said after a moment.

He looked over at her. "For what?"

"For…you know, to get married," she said.

"Oh," he said simply, then took a drink of his beer. "Good."

He looked back out at the yard, and it took Maggie a second to regroup.

"Ok. So, okay? You'll marry me, then?"

He looked back at her. "What?"

Maggie's mouth hung open just a little. "Are you going to marry me or what?"

"Well, no."

Maggie blinked a few times. "You said if I proposed, you would say yes."

"Oh, was that a proposal?" Wyatt asked, looking almost convincingly surprised.

Maggie thought about heaving him over the rail, but she knew she lacked the leverage. "Yeah," she snapped.

"Really? Because it sounded more like you were asking me if I wanted cheddar or Muenster on my burger," he said.

"We're having spaghetti," she said.

Wyatt turned around in his chair, stretched out his ridiculously long legs, and rested his beer in his lap.

"How did David propose to you?" he asked, like he was interviewing her for a talk show.

"I don't—we started talking about getting married when we were fourteen, Wyatt," she said snippily. "I don't think he did propose."

"Of course not," Wyatt said. "Well, I don't need you to get all fancy about it, and I don't think it's necessary for it to be dramatic or even particularly romantic, but it ought to at least be noticeable."

Maggie popped her fists back onto her hips. So many replies came to mind that she couldn't decide on one. "You're an ass," she said, which generally served as her default.

"Yeah, well, dead horse and all that," he said, and took another drink of his beer as she stalked back around the corner of the house. Then he grinned out at the yard.

⚓ ⚓ ⚓

Later that night, Maggie sat at the table on the deck, the Corzo file from Mike, and her own case file open in front of her and a half-full glass of wine beside her. She took notes longhand, as was her habit, as she went through each page in Mike's folder. The wind had died down a bit with the setting of the sun, and now, at close to one in the morning, all was quiet, save for the occasional rustle of leaves or the perambulations of a coon or possum.

The receipts from Marisol's bathroom weren't of much interest. They were both from her secured card. One was for the trip she and Axel had made to the Marathon station Wednesday night. The other was from Café con Leche earlier that day.

There really wasn't anything else from the lab that Maggie didn't already know. The cigarette butts outside bothered her, though. Either someone who liked the same brand had been smoking for some time near where Marisol was murdered, or she had had some reason to go outside to smoke, even though she'd been smoking in her room. The credit card and the missing iPhone were another problem Maggie didn't like.

Her own phone interrupted her thoughts as it vibrated on the table. It was Axel. Maggie picked it up and connected.

"Hey," she said.

"Hey," Axel answered. He sounded like he was outdoors.

"Where are you?" Maggie asked him.

"Out off of the Cut."

"Are you working?" Maggie asked, taken aback.

"No, just sitting," he answered. His words were just a hair slow.

"Are you drinking?" she asked him gently.

"That, too."

"Axel."

"Come on, Maggie," he said, and she could hear him smile. "You know good and well that I'm a better captain drunk than most people are sober."

That was primarily true, but it wasn't the whole of the point.

"Do you want some company?" Maggie asked. "I can grab Daddy's runabout."

"No, this is company enough," Axel said quietly.

"Are you okay?"

"Yeah," he answered, but he didn't try hard to make it sound true. "I just needed some time on the water. Everything's clearer out on the water. You know that."

"Yeah."

"I just wanted to check in and see what's going on. With Mari."

"Well, actually, I tried to call you earlier," Maggie said. "Her boyfriend's here."

"Is that a fact?"

"I don't think it'll actually be anything, but I'd appreciate it if you just kind of laid low, you know?"

"Why?" he asked, but it wasn't really a question.

"I don't know what his deal is," Maggie answered. "But on the off-chance that he thinks you killed Marisol, I don't want some kind of incident."

"What's his name?" he asked her.

"Forget it, Axel."

"Does he think I killed her?"

"I don't know. He knows you were arrested," she said.

"Maybe he knows I didn't kill her. Maybe he did."

Maggie sighed. "Look, that's a possibility, but so far we don't know that he wasn't in Tampa when she was killed. He says he didn't know she was here."

"She said she was here for him, Maggie," Axel said.

"I know."

"What's he like?"

"He's an ass," Maggie answered. "Sizable ego. Not all that bright."

"And you think he might come looking for me?"

"Not really. I just want you to be aware," Maggie answered. "And it would be helpful to me if you kept a low profile."

Axel was quiet for a moment. Maggie could just hear the water lapping against his hull. It made her think she could smell a hint of salt.

"Axel, I don't want you looking for him, either, okay?" He didn't answer. "Axel."

"I heard you," he said. "I spent some time researching strangulation today," he said after a moment.

"Axel," Maggie said, sighing.

"In the movies, they make it look so quick," he said. "But it's not, really, is it?"

Maggie swallowed. "Not necessarily."

"A lot depends on the strength of the one doing the strangling," he went on quietly. "And the victims don't really pass out peacefully beforehand, do they?"

"Sometimes they lose consciousness," Maggie said.

"Sometimes they don't," he said.

Maggie didn't answer, and he was quiet for a moment. Maggie heard him take a drink. Bourbon, most likely, from the aluminum travel mug she and David had given him for his birthday some years back.

Maggie looked out across the tops of the trees that covered most of her land, in the direction of the bay. She squinted, as though she would be able to see his running lights miles away out there on the water.

"I read that it's common for victims to lose control of their bowels and bladders while they're being strangled," Axel said quietly. "Is that true?"

Maggie took in a slow breath. "Sometimes."

"Did Mari mess herself, Maggie?" His voice was so soft she would have strained to hear him if she hadn't already known what he would ask.

"No," she lied.

They were quiet for a moment.

Maggie felt her eyes warm and water, and she blinked a few times. "I can come out there, Axel," she said gently.

"No. I'm okay, Maggie," he said. "I'll talk to you tomorrow, okay?"

He disconnected without waiting for her to answer, and she put down the phone and stared out at the dark woods behind her house.

She jumped just a little when the sliding glass door beside her slid open. Sky was standing there in a pair of knit shorts and a tee shirt, her hair up in a messy bun.

"Dude, it's like one in the morning," Sky said quietly.

"I couldn't sleep," Maggie said. "What are you doing up?"

"I had to use the bathroom."

Maggie looked just like her mother, and Sky looked just like Maggie, with the exception of a charming cleft chin. They had always assumed it came from David's side of the family, but Maggie found herself staring at Sky lately, looking for resemblances to Boudreaux. She hadn't really found any.

"Is that stuff from Uncle Axel's case?" Sky asked.

"Yeah." Maggie took a sip of her wine.

"That's such bull," Sky said.

"I know."

"Is he okay?"

Maggie shrugged. "I just talked to him," she said. "He's out on the boat."

"He's working?"

"No, he just wanted to be out on the water," Maggie answered. She understood that.

"I hate this," Sky said quietly.

"Me, too." Maggie put her pen down. "I didn't get to ask you, how was the Gainesville visit?"

"I think college would be a lot more appetizing if there weren't so many college-age guys there," Sky said. "Guys really shouldn't even be allowed to speak in public until they're like thirty."

Maggie smiled at her. "You could always go up north, to some girls' college," she said, though she knew Sky wanted to stay close, and that was perfectly fine with her.

"Yeah, except I don't really like girls that much, either," Sky said. "I guess I get my social skills from you."

"FSU wasn't so bad," Maggie said. Maggie had gotten her BA there.

"Yeah, I'm leaning that way. Bella still wants me to go to Auburn with her, but I'm not into it."

"It would look good on your law school apps," Maggie said.

"I know. It's just so…inland," Sky said.

Maggie smiled at her daughter. "It is that."

"Of course, Wyatt thinks I should go there so I can get Iron Bowl tickets," Sky said.

"He'll forgive you if you don't," Maggie said. "Just do what feels right to you, Sky. You know I'm behind you."

Sky nodded. "I know." She looked down at the deck for a moment, tapping her thigh with her fingers, then looked back up at Maggie. "I feel better about leaving, you know, 'cause of you and Wyatt Earp."

Maggie smiled. "Were you worried about me?"

"Well, I mean…you and your umbilical cord, you know?"

"Yeah, I know," Maggie answered. "It's fine Sky. It's not like I thought I could keep you at home forever." Maggie felt a tightness in her chest. Actually, she had hoped she could. "Besides, you'll be back."

It was Sky's intention to work for the State's Attorney's office in Franklin County. That had been Maggie's dream, too, at one time.

"Yeah. Meanwhile, you still have the dweeb," Sky said. "I'm pretty sure he's going to college online in his room."

"We'll see," Maggie said, smiling.

"I'm going to bed," Sky said. "By the way, Stoopid's roosting on the ceiling fan again."

Maggie sighed. "Turn it on. He'll get down."

"Yeah, while he's crapping like a Spirograph all over the living room. Night Mom."

"Goodnight, baby."

Maggie watched her go back inside, sliding the door shut behind her. Then she looked out in the general direction of the bay, several miles away.

She thought about Axel sitting out there under the stars, listening to the water lap at his hull, probably drinking bourbon, and she wished he didn't have to go off by himself to feel like he wasn't alone.

FOURTEEN

Sunday dawned clear and vaguely cool, at least by Florida standards. Maggie had gone to bed with the sincere intention of sleeping in until at least seven, but was jerked awake by something that sounded like a goat being eaten butt-first by a snake.

She bolted upright and kicked at the covers until Stoopid choked mid-crow and flapped indignantly down to the floor. Maggie swung her legs over the side of the bed, picked up her phone and saw that it was after six, and decided to get up anyway.

She tossed Stoopid out onto the deck with a bowl of vegetable scraps so that she could have her coffee in peace, then took her second cup with her when she went out to tend to the chickens. Stoopid followed, this being the only time of day that he remembered he had a flock. He might have taken a shine to sitting on upholstered furniture, but he still loved some chicken feed and, on occasion, some chicken love.

Maggie let the birds out into their fenced yard, fed and watered them, gathered nine eggs, and then closed the fence with Stoopid still in there. He'd fly back over it eventually, but it gave her a certain satisfaction. She knew it would be short lived; the next time she saw him, he'd probably be playing on the XBox.

Once she'd washed the eggs and put them in her grandmother's big stoneware bowl, she fixed herself another cup of coffee and sat down at the rustic dining room table her father had built with his father.

As she drank her coffee, she ran her hand along the table's age-worn surface. She picked at the nick from the time Kyle had accidentally dropped David's hammer. She looked for and found the tiny "S" that Sky had carved onto the edge when she was eleven. Smiled at the word "Dad" that had been poorly scratched into the varnish in front of David's old place. Sky had only been six then, and hadn't meant any harm. Like Maggie, she had been a Daddy's girl.

Maggie looked at it for a long while, then picked up her phone and dialed.

⚓ ⚓ ⚓

Bennett Boudreaux put down the weekly newspaper and poured himself another cup of Café du Monde from the Lenox coffee pot. Over at the island in the middle of the large, bright kitchen, his Creole cook and housekeeper, Amelia, stood staring into a cast iron skillet, where one over-medium egg gently sizzled.

Boudreaux stirred a spoonful of sand-colored cane sugar into his coffee, then took a sip. Amelia looked over at him, then put one hand on her hip.

"I seen you sittin' up all hours on the back porch last night," she said to him.

He glanced over at her as he set his cup down, then picked up his paper. "I couldn't sleep," he said.

"You can't sleep a lot these days," she said.

He looked up to find her still staring at him. She was only two years older than he, and her mother had raised them both. There were many people who were afraid to be frank with him. She wasn't any of those people.

"Everything's fine, Amelia," he said.

"Lie to me all you want, Mr. Benny," Amelia said. "But you keep hangdoggin' around like you doin', she gon' pick up on it."

"I'll deal with Miss Evangeline," Boudreaux said.

"Go 'head then," she said, jerking her head at the back door. "There she go."

Boudreaux sighed and stood up from the table. A moment later, the back door opened, and an aluminum walker outfitted with bright green tennis balls came clattering through, followed closely by Boudreaux's one hundred year old former nanny. At less than five feet and fewer than ninety pounds, she almost disappeared within her flowered housedress. A bright bandana, yellow today, covered her small oval head and helped keep her thick glasses in place.

"Mornin', Mama," Amelia said as she slid the egg onto a plate that held one slice of bacon and a piece of sourdough toast.

"Mornin', baby," the old woman answered. Her voice sounded like nutmeg being grated.

"Good morning, Miss Evangeline," Boudreaux said, as she crept toward the table.

"We see," she said.

Boudreaux pulled out her chair and waited. Once she was abreast of him, he kissed one of her hollowed cheeks, then stood by until she'd managed to arrange herself in her seat. He sat back down on his side of the table as Amelia set Miss Evangeline's plate and hot tea in front of her.

The old woman inspected the plate, which was precisely the same as every plate she'd inspected for the last twelve-thousand mornings, then poked her Coke bottle lenses in Boudreaux's direction.

"Them cat from next door was fornicatin' under my window again last night," she barked. "I need you give me back my buzzer."

Boudreaux sighed as he put his cup down. "I was on the porch quite late last night, and I didn't hear anything."

"That's cause you ain't sleep under my window, no," she said. "Where my buzzer at?"

"I'll give it back to you later," he said, which was a lie. Her days of carrying a Taser were over. He'd gotten it for her protection, and taken it away for everyone else's. He picked the paper back up and had twelve seconds of quiet in which to read it.

"What the purple place on the paper?" Boudreaux heard her ask.

"The Apalachicola River Inn," he answered quietly. "They found a woman's body in the creek. Or I should say a gator found it."

Miss Evangeline's head popped up, the sunlight bouncing off of her lenses. "Gator? What she doin' messin' with the gator?"

"It doesn't sound like she was doing much of anything," Boudreaux said as he turned the page.

"Gator ain't no puppy dog, no," she said snapped. "Cain't go in his place like you belong there."

Boudreaux sighed and let the paper drop to the table as he picked up his coffee. "She didn't go for a dip," he said. "Apparently, her body was dumped there."

She was quiet for a moment, and Boudreaux picked his paper back up. After a moment, he heard her sandpaper voice from beyond the editorial page.

"That ain't how you do it, no," she said. "You take the body out the swamp, weigh it down good."

"I'll keep that in mind," he answered quietly.

"What they gon' do the gator?"

"Euthanize it, I expect," he said.

"Do what the gator?"

"Kill it," he said.

It was a few moments before she spoke again. He'd almost thought he'd have the rest of his coffee in peace when she piped back up.

"I need you go get me the gator," she said. "We put him the next door yard. Them cat won't be fornicatin' under my window anymore, no."

He was about to make a smart remark when his phone buzzed on the table beside his coffee. He didn't ordinarily take calls during breakfast, but he recognized Maggie's number. He connected the call.

"Hello, Maggie," he said quietly. Out of the corner of his eye, he saw Miss Evangeline's head jerk up.

"Hello, Mr. Boudreaux," Maggie said, her voice even.

Boudreaux waited a moment. He heard her sigh.

"I was wondering if we could talk sometime today," she said finally. "Tonight, actually."

"Is this about your case?" he asked.

"No."

He took a slow breath and let it out silently. "Come over anytime."

"I—" Maggie started.

"Tell the girl tomorrow ice cream day," Miss Evangeline barked before Maggie could finish. Boudreaux looked up at her. "She come take me the ice cream."

"She'll take you nowhere," he said quietly.

"You ain't the boss o' her, no," Miss Evangeline snapped back.

Boudreaux ignored her, looked out the window across the room. The wind was brisk, and the palm outside was almost panicky.

"I'm sorry, Maggie," he said quietly. "You were saying?"

"I'd rather talk someplace more private," she said.

Boudreaux thought about that a moment. "I could use some time out on the island," he said. "You know where my house is, on Schooner?"

"Yes."

"Will you come there?"

"Yes," she answered after a moment.

"What time shall I meet you?"

"About seven," she said.

"I'll see you then, Maggie," he said gently.

She hung up without answering, and he put the phone down on the table. Miss Evangeline was staring at him.

"Girl know," she said.

"Yes," he said.

"You tell her?"

"No, she just knows," he answered quietly, his eyes on the window and his thoughts somewhere else entirely.

"What time we go the ice cream?"

Boudreaux sighed and looked back at the old woman.. "How about two? That way when she arrests you for

Tasering some other halfwit, the newspaper will have time to report that I was seen posting bail for my nanny."

He gave her a tight smile, and she sat up a bit straighter. He thought perhaps he could hear her spine creaking.

"Go on, smile at me like you do, Mr. Benny," she said. "You ain't gon' smile when I pull your lip up over your head, no."

⚓ ⚓ ⚓

Maggie spent the day enjoying some time with the kids. They spent most of it fishing off of Lafayette Pier, then picnicking in Lafayette Park beneath one of the old, stately trees.

Maggie tried to distract herself with the banter of her kids, the fight in the fish they caught, the way the sunlight shattered into a million diamonds on the bay, but underneath it all was a gently pulsing dread of the evening ahead.

Sky had plans for the evening with her friends and Kyle had a sleepover. After she dropped him off just after 5pm, she felt at loose ends. She considered stopping by Wyatt's for some support and fortitude, but suspected she'd chicken out of going to Boudreaux's if she did. She thought about grabbing a coffee, but she was nervous enough.

In the end, she decided to head over to the island early. All of her life, whenever she'd needed to be soothed or strengthened, she'd gone to the beach. Staring out at the Gulf, listening to the waves, being reminded how small she and her problems really were, these things calmed her more than anything else she knew.

Boudreaux's house was at the quiet, eastern end of St. George Island, where there were far fewer homes and fewer of them were rented out to tourists. She'd never been to his beach house, but she'd seen him there once over the summer, on a warmer and far more frightening night.

She parked in the partially developed lot next door, and glanced at his driveway as she made her way down to the beach. She didn't see his car, and she was glad he hadn't come early as well. She'd already spent enough time trying to figure out all of the things she wanted to say and all of the things she didn't, but she wanted some time to try not to think at all.

There was no one else on the beach, which wasn't surprising. The crowds from the seafood festival at the beginning of the month were gone, and the tourists who were left were at the other end of the island.

The tide was headed back in, and Maggie kicked off her flip-flops and walked through the soft, dry sand and onto the packed, damp sand closer to the water. The water was a deep green in the waning light, topped with grayish-white froth as it unfolded itself onto the shore.

She sat down on the sand and watched the water, watched as the sky went from silver to orange to a deep, inscrutable blue. Now and then, she saw the lights of a shrimp boat as it headed out for the night, and she tried not to imagine that one of them might be David, granted a pass for a night of fishing back on earth, simply because he'd loved it so.

After some time, when the beach had gone dark except for the moonlight, Maggie walked down to the shore and stood at the edge of the now black water. She closed her eyes and breathed deeply as she heard each wave break onto the beach, as she felt them course over her feet. She almost smiled as she felt the wet sand shift underneath her, pulled toward the Gulf by the receding water. It was one of her favorite sensations.

"Hello, Maggie."

Maggie started just a bit, then looked over her shoulder.

Boudreaux was standing about six feet behind her. He, too, had taken off his shoes. The bottoms of his khaki cargo pants were sandy. The wind made ripples in his black cashmere sweater and tossed his hair over his brow.

"You're early," Maggie said.

"So are you."

They stared at each other long enough for it to become uncomfortable. Maggie was grateful that the wind was blowing her hair into her face. She had never had a poker face, and she felt like her hair offered a curtain behind which to hide emotions she didn't feel like sharing.

Eventually, Boudreaux sighed quietly. "Maggie, I'm sorry. You should have been told a long time ago," he said.

"Why are you in my life now?" Maggie asked him. "If everybody was so okay with keeping this a secret, why did you start this now?"

He looked at her for a moment before answering. "Once we started talking, I didn't want to stop," he said.

"You should have told me the truth!" she snapped.

"Yes." His eyes pinned her to nothing. "If I had, what would you have done?"

She thought about that a moment. "Probably exactly what I'm doing now," she said angrily. "But at least I wouldn't—" She broke off and looked away, unsure how she meant to finish that sentence. At least she wouldn't have felt so betrayed? No, she would have no matter when she'd been told.

"Wouldn't what?" he asked quietly.

She looked back at him, standing there so calmly. She wanted to seem that calm but she just didn't have the energy to make the effort. "At least I wouldn't feel like such an idiot," she said.

"Why should you feel like an idiot?" he asked her quietly. "For not knowing?"

"For caring so much!" she yelled without meaning to.

"Caring about what?"

Maggie opened her mouth to answer, then shook her head and looked out at the water. "This was a mistake," she said. "I'm not ready to have this conversation with you."

"Yes, you are," she heard him say. "You just don't want to be so transparent about it."

Maggie's head shot back around. "Somebody'd better be transparent about it, because it isn't any of you! I feel like such an ass! All the angst I went though, trying to tell right from wrong, all the crap I put up with for talking to you, because I felt some kind of connection to you."

"That connection is real," he said.

"That connection is crap!" she yelled. "All of those conversations, you putting your *life* on the line to save me, meant nothing. It was just you working off some kind of obligation! You and your Catholic guilt."

"Of course I felt some kind of obligation, Maggie!" Boudreaux snapped. "How could I not? My own nephew raped you! Do you have any idea what that did to my mind?"

"How can you even make this about you?" Maggie yelled. "That had nothing to do with you, and I don't want your damn penance!"

Boudreaux reached out to touch her shoulder, and she jerked her body away from him.

"Maggie—" he started.

"No," she shot out, and when he reached out again, she swept up her arm and blocked him as though he were about to strike her. He twisted his arm around hers and jerked her close.

"Do you think for one minute that that pathetic little worm would have laid a hand on you if he'd known who you were?" he snarled. "He would have been afraid to breathe your air!"

Maggie swept her arm in a circle and released it from his. "I don't want your reparations, Mr. Boudreaux," she said evenly.

"I don't care whether you want them or not," he said, his eyes narrowed. "It would never have happened to you if I had claimed you from the beginning."

"I'm not your lost luggage!" Maggie said, hating that her voice was becoming shrill, that heat and moisture were building in her eyes.

"No, you're my daughter!" he shot back. "And I may not be your daddy, but I am your father!"

Maggie had no idea she was going to strike him, but she watched her fist as it landed, halfheartedly, on his chest.

"You were my *friend*!"

She saw him flinch, not from the physical blow, but from her words.

"I'm still your friend!" he yelled back.

"Do you have any idea, any idea at all, how stupid I feel?" she asked him, tears stinging her eyes. "I thought I was so damn special, with my intimate friendship with the enigmatic Bennett Boudreaux. I fought for it, dammit! I fought for some relationship that only I was having!"

Boudreaux reached out and gently, but firmly, grasped her shoulders. "Listen to me—"

Maggie shook her head. "No. I don't want to hear any more."

"Listen anyway," he said more forcefully.

Maggie started to twist away, and Boudreaux tightened his grasp. She jerked away, and felt herself lose her balance, felt the earth kip sideways. She stumbled backward a few steps, overcompensated as the incoming waves pushed against the backs of her legs, and then she fell backwards, into the cold, dark water.

She thrashed for just a moment, panic engulfing her as tangibly as the water did, but then she found her feet and stood, gasping. It was only about three and a half feet deep, and not especially rough, but she had to work at keeping her footing.

"Maybe now you can cool off enough to listen to what I have to say," Boudreaux said, his hands on his hips.

Maggie barely heard him over the pounding of her blood in her ears. She slowly lowered her arms, her palms parallel to the surface, as though she could calm everything that was in the water with her, as though she could stop it from coming.

"Ever since that first day at Boss Oyster, every moment I have spent with you I spent because I wanted to know you," Boudreaux said, pointing a finger at her. "Because I like being with you. I *need* to be with you," he said.

Maggie registered that he was speaking, but failed to understand what he was saying.

She could feel them around her in the water, behind and beside her. She slowly turned in a circle, trying to see blacker spots in the black water, trying desperately not to be surprised by the movement, by the bump, by the shadow she knew was coming.

When she had turned full circle, she tried to make her legs propel her forward, toward the sand that was just a few feet away. Toward Boudreaux. But her feet wouldn't move again. Stillness was as close to invisibility as she could get, and she clung to it despite her desperate need to be back on the sand. She looked at Boudreaux, her eyes wide, her mouth wider.

He opened his mouth to continue speaking, then closed it as his own eyes narrowed. "Damn it!" he said, then half-ran into the water and scooped her up. "Damn it!" he said again.

He carried her back onto the shore and set her down. She took a big gulp of air, stopped herself from sitting down on the firm, damp sand. She didn't want to lean in when Boudreaux pulled her to his chest, but she couldn't help it. She folded her arms across her own chest, assembled at least that barrier between them.

"Are you afraid of the water?" he asked incredulously.

"No!" Maggie barked, and pulled away from him. She glanced up at him, then looked away. "Yes."

"But you love the Gulf," he said quietly.

"I know that!" she snapped. "I just can't get in it anymore."

"Since when?"

She glanced back at him, her eyes slits. "Since I was fifteen," she said.

CHAPTER FIFTEEN

Maggie sat on the top step of Boudreaux's back deck, wrapped in a white bathrobe that was several sizes too big.

Beyond the circle of light cast by the deck's lights, Maggie could see the thin whitecaps as the waves threw themselves onto the sand. The waves were the only sound that disturbed the evening until Maggie heard Boudreaux's footsteps as he came out through the sliding glass door.

She swallowed and turned her head to look down the beach, although there was nothing to see, as he settled one step below her on the other side of the stairs. He was a silent for a moment before he spoke.

"Maggie," he said.

Reluctantly, she looked over at him. He was holding two glass mugs, and extended one to her. Wisps of steam rose from the cup and quickly dissolved into the chilly air.

"What is it?" Maggie asked, though she didn't actually care.

"Hot tea." He raised the cup another inch, and she reached out and took it with both hands. The warmth was welcome, and she was glad for something to do with her hands other than twisting the ties of his robe.

Boudreaux took a sip of his tea and waited. Maggie finally raised the cup and took a swallow. The tea was hot and bitter, but it felt good going down. She nestled the cup in her lap and looked out at the water, pretending she didn't know that Boudreaux was staring at her.

Finally the silence, and unanswered questions, became too frustrating.

"Why did you suddenly decide that you wanted to know me?" she asked. When she looked over at him, he was still staring. It took him a moment to answer.

"I don't think I did," he said. "I feel like it was decided for me." Maggie raised an eyebrow at him, and he sighed. "When Gregory told me what he'd done, I realized that all of the justification I'd done, the rationalization that you were better off outside my life, was all just a bunch of self-serving pretext. It didn't keep you from being hurt by the Boudreaux family, did it?"

Maggie felt the anger swirling in her stomach again. "Are you trying to say you sacrificed your fatherhood to protect me, Mr. Boudreaux?" she asked.

"No, of course not," he answered quietly. "I didn't have room in my life for you or your mother, not that she actually wanted a place in it."

Maggie looked away, not wanting to watch the words about her mother actually come out of his mouth.

"I've tried to give you my financial support, Maggie, tried to do what I could to help, but I didn't want to be your father."

Maggie could feel the anger climbing up her throat, but she was tired of being so angry. Exhausted from it. "And yet here we are," she said quietly.

"Yes."

She heard the gentle rustling of his expensive trousers, saw in her peripheral vision that he was leaning toward her. She turned to look at him as he rested his elbows on his knees.

"After that day that we first sat together at Boss Oyster, I would have wanted to know you, even if you weren't my daughter," he said. His blue eyes were locked on hers, brilliant in their intensity, and even though the closeness bothered her, she couldn't look away, either. "I need you to understand that, Maggie."

"Why?"

"Because it matters," he said simply.

"To you?"

"I think it matters to both of us," he said.

He was right, and the fact that he knew it made her blink a few times to hide her discomfort.

"We've both lived in this town all of my life," she said. "You were there many times, when I was with Daddy, bringing in a load. But you never thought about me until your nephew told you he raped me."

"That's not wholly true," he said. He took a swallow of his tea before he went on. "It would be nice to say that I have a drawer full of newspaper clippings and school pictures at home. I don't. But I did watch you sometimes, and sometimes I wished that things had been different. I would see you at softball and baseball games and think how beautiful you were becoming, how strong and independent you seemed." He paused for a moment, his eyes seeming to search hers. "I would wonder sometimes if you were anything like me."

Maggie looked away then. If he saw any similarities, she wasn't ready to hear about it.

"I have a great deal of respect for Gray," he said after a moment. "He did something I never would have done, probably couldn't have done. But I've always been envious of him as well."

Maggie looked at him. "Because of my mother?" she asked, and tasted the bitterness in her tone.

"No," he said quietly, and held her with those eyes. "I wish I could tell you that I was in love with your mother, but I wasn't. I didn't even know her, and she didn't fit into my plans. Neither did her child. Not then."

Maggie looked away for a moment. What he was saying hurt, and she could show him her anger, but she'd rather be shot than show him her pain. "Do you know what it's like to wake up one day and not even know your nationality?" she snapped. "Half of everything I've ever thought about my family, my heritage, is false, and now there's just a blank space where it used to be."

Boudreaux was quiet for a moment. He took a sip of his tea before answering. Maggie's had grown cool in her hands.

"My father's people were true Acadians," he said finally. "They immigrated to Nova Scotia from France, and were relocated to Louisiana during the Great Expulsion in the 1700s. My mother was a first generation American. Her parents moved to Louisiana in the forties, from A Illa de Arousa, an island off the northwestern coast of Spain."

Maggie looked at him. "Spanish?" She had a hard time adjusting her ideas about her own genetic makeup.

"Yes." Boudreaux drained his cup and set it down carefully on the step beside him before he looked at her. "You have her laugh, you know." Maggie blinked at him a few times. "Your daughter has her chin. I was barely more than a toddler when she died, but I remember her very clearly. She was an exceptionally beautiful woman."

His voice had grown very quiet, and Maggie saw his eyes darken as he spoke.

"How did she die?"

Boudreaux swallowed. "You don't need to know about that," he said.

"I'm a little tired of the stuff people think I don't need to know, Mr. Boudreaux," she said evenly.

He reached up and smoothed his eyebrow with his little finger. "My father killed her," he said, his voice quiet and his tone somehow matter-of-fact. "The official word was that she fell out of my father's *pirogue* while they were night fishing on Bayou Petit Caillou, but he killed her."

"How do you know?" Maggie asked.

"Everyone knew," he answered. "But it was Southern Louisiana in the 1950s, and she was a spic married to a coonass. No one cared."

His voice was calm, but Maggie recognized the anger beneath his even tone. "I'm surprised you didn't kill him," she said softly.

"I probably would have eventually, but he had the heart attack," he said mildly. "I admit to feeling somewhat inconvenienced by that."

Suddenly their conversation felt very much like so many others, and Maggie felt in danger of becoming comfortable with it. She looked away from him, looked back out at the beach and listened to the wind rustling through the sea oats.

After a moment, she heard him shift beside her. "Why are you afraid of the water?"

She sighed. "I'm not afraid of water. Just the Gulf, and the ocean. The damn sharks."

"Why?"

She looked over at him. He was so close, just a foot away, and even in the faint light of the deck his eyes shone blue and sharp and clear.

"What difference does it make?" she asked him wearily.

"You're terrified of something you clearly love," he said. "I want to know why."

She took a good mouthful of her tea before she answered. She didn't want to share anything with him, yet she always had. The pull was just as strong as it had always been. "I explained it to you once," she said finally. "I'm afraid of a lot of things. Ever since…the rape. I saw a psychologist a few times, years ago. She said that it's because I found out that really scary things don't just happen to other people. Apparently, it's not uncommon for people with PTSD to develop fears they never had before."

Boudreaux studied her for a moment. "So, you have PTSD," he said.

"Yes," Maggie answered with a shrug.

"From the rape," he said.

Maggie looked back at him. "Don't try to claim that as another cross for you to bear," she said eveny.

"I don't like to think of you being scared of anything," he said.

"Then don't," she said, but not unkindly.

They sat in silence for a moment, Maggie watching the surf and Boudreaux watching her.

"Well, you certainly scared me," he said finally. "The other night. Had you considered just asking me straight out?"

Maggie just managed to not roll her eyes, but only barely. "Yes. But you'd had plenty of time to tell me yourself."

"That's true. I almost did, more than once," he said.

"Why didn't you?"

Boudreaux looked at her a moment, scratched gently at his eyebrow, then stood up, pulling a pewter cigarette case from his shirt pocket. "I saved my evening cigarette for later," he said. "Do you mind?"

She shook her head.

⚓ ⚓ ⚓

Several hundred feet away, beneath the back deck of an empty house, a lighter rasped and a red glow flared and then dimmed as a cigarette was lit. The smoker tucked the cigarettes and lighter back into his jacket pocket, then exhaled and leaned against the deck support, squinting through the smoke at Maggie and Boudreaux on the back stairs.

They were too far away to be heard clearly, but he didn't care much about their conversation.

⚓ ⚓ ⚓

Boudreaux dipped his head toward his cupped palm, and lit his cigarette. He exhaled slowly, away from Maggie, then leaned back against the handrail.

"Gray wanted to be the one to tell you," he said. "I thought I owed him that much." He took another drag of his cigarette before speaking again. "There was some selfishness there, too," he said.

Maggie looked over at him, and he took a moment to go on.

"I was a little afraid that you might never speak to me again," he said finally. You have every right to be angry with me."

Maggie looked back out at the water. "I know that," she said, her tone harsher than she meant it to be. She looked back at him, craned her neck to look up into those blue eyes as he studied her calmly. Then she sighed. "I am angry with you. I tried to be angrier."

"I don't understand what that means," he said.

Maggie felt the frustration bubbling up again somewhere around her lungs. She looked out at the dark. "If it had been anyone else…if it hadn't been you, you're the one I would have gone to talk to about it."

He didn't respond, and after a moment she looked back at him. His brows were drawn together, his incredible eyes kind.

"Why do you suppose that is?" he asked gently.

She stood up quickly. "You know damn well why," she answered.

"Yes, I do," he said. "Because that connection has been there from the beginning, regardless of why."

"I don't know how to relate to you anymore," she said.

"Maggie, I don't need to be your father," his voice quiet. "The way we were was good enough. Let's just be what we've always been."

Maggie swallowed hard, torn between putting her head on his chest and slapping him down the stairs.

"My clothes should be dry," she said. "I need to go."

"Maggie—" he started, but she was already inside.

A few minutes later, she stepped back out onto the deck in her own clothes. Boudreaux turned around and leaned against the rail as she stopped at the top of the deck stairs. He waited for her to speak, and she waited to come up with something she felt comfortable saying.

"Thank you for meeting me out here, Mr. Boudreaux," was what she managed finally.

He seemed about to say something, then scratched gently at his eyebrow for a moment. "It's always good to see you, Maggie," he said instead.

Maggie was standing less than two feet away from Boudreaux. She could see the tiny lines that radiated from the corners of each of his beautiful eyes, just catch the scent of his cologne. She could almost see herself laying her cheek against his chest for a moment, and she could tell from his expression that he could almost see that, too.

Instead, she started down the stairs. She had hit the sand by the time he spoke.

"Maggie."

She stopped and turned around, looked up at him.

"Your new sheriff, Curtis Bledsoe," he said. "You need to be very careful around him"

That wasn't any of the things she had expected him to say. "Why?"

"If Governor Spaulding appointed him, he had his reasons. None of them could be good."

"I thought you were friends with all the Governors of Florida," Maggie said.

"Not this one," Boudreaux answered.

"Anything I should know?" Maggie asked.

"Yes," Boudreaux answered smoothly. "And I just told you."

Maggie chewed the corner of her lip a moment her mind forming questions that he probably wouldn't answer. "Okay," she said finally, then started through the sand. "Goodnight, Mr. Boudreaux."

"Goodnight, Maggie," he answered.

⚓ ⚓ ⚓

Beneath the empty house down the beach, the watcher saw Maggie start away from Boudreaux's house. He ground his cigarette out in the sand, then walked out the far side of the porch and headed back to the vehicle waiting across the road.

CHAPTER
SIXTEEN

The next morning, Maggie and Dwight pulled into the Sheriff's Office parking lot within seconds of each other. Maggie got out of her Cherokee with a fresh latte, two extra shots, from Apalachicola Coffee. Dwight walked up to her with a cup of gas station coffee in his hand. Ordinarily, she would have given him some crap about that, but she was too tired to make the effort.

"Hey, Maggie," Dwight said as he fell into step with her.

"Hey, Dwight. Did you get anything on the grand opening thing?"

"Yeah, sorta," he answered. "He was definitely there. The thing started at lunchtime, regular opening hours for the place. It's some kinda fancy tapas bar or something."

"Okay."

"The party lasted til like five or so, til it was time for them to get ready for dinner," Dwight continued. "But I can't find anybody that remembers seeing him for sure after about three."

Maggie stopped walking, and he stopped short beside her, watched her as she took a drink of her coffee.

"So, he could have been here by eight or so," she said.

"Looks like."

"Call around, see if any of the hotels had him registered that night," she said as she started walking again. "Maybe he's that stupid."

"Already done it. He ain't," Dwight said as he caught up with her. "Either that or he wasn't here."

"Did you find anything out about the rental car?"

"Not yet," he answered. "I only got a partial on the plate, but we're running what we got. I haven't seen the car around, have you?"

"No." Maggie gnawed the corner of her lip for a moment. "What about her car? Is it still here?"

"Yeah, I told her brother we'd call him when we were done with it," Dwight answered.

"Do me a favor and go over it, look in the nooks and crannies, see if the phone or the credit card turn up."

"Buggin' you," he said as he opened the door to the Sheriff's Office.

"Yeah," she answered.

"They might be back in Tampa, though," Dwight said.

Maggie nodded. "Good point."

"I'll look anyway," he said, as he headed in one direction and she went the other. Her destination was the office she still considered Wyatt's, to see the man she still considered not Wyatt by a long shot.

When she arrived in Bledsoe's open doorway, he was on the phone. He glanced up at her and held up a hand. She waited for a moment until he finished the call and waved her in. She noticed for the first time that he'd traded Wyatt's worn in old desk chair, and she couldn't help wondering if it was so his feet could touch the floor.

"What can I do for you, Lieutenant?" he asked, without sounding like he wanted an answer.

"The Corzo case," she replied. "The boyfriend, Toby Mann, insists he didn't know she was even here, but I'm not sure I buy that. He put her on one of his credit cards. I'd like to see about getting a warrant to pull the records, see if she made any charges on it that would have let him know where she was. The card's missing."

"No," he said simply.

"No, why?"

"Do you have any probable cause to get a warrant on him?"

"The guy's her boyfriend. A drug dealer," she answered. "She was with another man."

"Another man who was on the scene," he replied. "As opposed to a boyfriend that witnesses put in Tampa that afternoon."

"That *afternoon*," she said, trying hard to keep her face impassive and her tone even.

"He also came up here voluntarily to speak with us," Bledsoe said, tidying his already-tidy desk as though he were preparing for some other, more important business once he got rid of Maggie. "As of now, you don't have anything that's going to compel a judge to issue a warrant for this guy's credit card records."

"I think Judge Greer might," Maggie responded, then couldn't help herself. "He seemed to think Axel shouldn't have been charged based on what we have so far."

Bledsoe folded his arms across his chest and regarded her with a tight smile that she imagined was supposed to be intimidating. It wasn't. "Is that right?" he asked. "But you have even less on this guy Mann. In fact, you have nothing, outside of him being a known felon. And I'm not about to start building a reputation as a department that asks the court for warrants willy-nilly."

Apparently, willy-nilly arrests were okay with him. Maggie swallowed the words. He seemed to mistake her silence for having put her in her place, because his smile became more genuine.

"I realize that you're supposed to be the darling of the SO, full-grade Lieutenant and all that, but you're not working for Wyatt Hamilton anymore."

In her mind, Maggie withdrew her weapon and shot his new little chair full of holes. "I was promoted to Lieutenant a year before Wyatt came here," she said instead, her voice calm and quiet. "Sir."

He waved off her answer, but looked annoyed at the correction. "Nevertheless, I'm sure Wyatt kept a pretty long leash on you due to your, uh, relationship. You and I have a different relationship.

Maggie silently thanked God for that, and refrained from asking Bledsoe if he'd slept with Governor Spaulding to get *his* job.

"I'm not going to allow my people free rein to overlook evidence, or the lack thereof, so they can further their own biases. Request denied. If you come up with anything tenable regarding Mann, then come back and talk to me about warrants."

"I'll do that," Maggie answered, then turned and walked out of his office. She stalked down the hall and around the corner, walked through Wyatt's doorway and shut the door. He was at his computer, typing with both of his typing fingers.

"Hey," he said cheerfully, then frowned. "What's up?"

Maggie leaned on his desk. "I need you to get your old job back."

"I don't think I can," he said. "Besides, it's only been a couple of weeks."

"He's a creep," Maggie said. "He needs to go."

Wyatt took a pull on his Mountain Dew. "Try to stay positive. Maybe he'll have a tragic accident on the monkey bars."

Maggie sighed. "He's not just a creep. Boudreaux said we need to watch out for him."

"Why, exactly?"

"Because of his connection to Spaulding."

"Boudreaux's connected to all of the politicos," he countered.

"No, not that one, apparently."

"What's the problem, specifically?" Wyatt asked, his brows embracing each other.

"He wasn't feeling specific," Maggie answered.

"Of course not."

Maggie heaved out a sigh and felt herself deflate. "He's determined to take the easy out and go for Axel," she said. "He's getting in the way of looking at Toby Mann. He won't let me try for a warrant to get his credit card records."

"You trying to put him here?"

"Either that or prove he could have known Mari was. She was an authorized user on one of his accounts."

Wyatt nodded, thinking. "Why don't you ask him for the records?"

"I'm not ready for him to know I'm looking at him," she answered. "He'll be more helpful if he thinks he's here to help."

"What about the other guy, the big dealer down in Tampa?"

"Still trying to find him. Which makes him look good for it, too, I know."

"Well, drug dealing aside, it's almost always the current or the ex," Wyatt said. "Problem is, you've got the boyfriend, the ex-boyfriend and the ex-husband. Messy."

"It wasn't Axel," Maggie said quietly. "He's married or dated every toxic or obnoxious woman in Franklin County. If he was the choking kind, he would have done it already."

⚓ ⚓ ⚓

Maggie sat at her desk, staring at the Palmettos outside her window. There was a good wind going, and the trees waved their arms like teenaged boys egging on a fight. It was past time to leave, almost dark, and she should be on her way home, but she was frozen in frustration.

Dwight had reported back that he'd scoured every inch of Marisol's car and found neither iPhone nor credit card. If it was only the phone that was missing, Maggie would assume that she'd had it with her when she was killed, and that it had ended up in Scipio Creek, too. Or that her killer had taken it.

But the credit card bothered her. Both were means that Toby Mann could have used to track Mari if he'd needed to. But if she'd been in Apalach to arrange some kind of deal for Toby, why would she bother to stash the phone and card? If she wasn't here on his behalf, then whose?

Maggie had just slumped back in her chair and blown a breath up at the ceiling when her desk phone rang. She sat up and answered.

"Redmond."

"Hey, Maggie, it's Mike."

"Hey, Mike. What's up?"

"I processed those Newport butts we found on the dock," he answered. "Four of them had her saliva on them. The rest didn't."

Maggie took a slow breath. "Do they match any butts from the room?" She didn't want to come right out and ask if they matched Axel's.

"No," he answered, and Maggie's sigh of relief was carefully silent. "You know I can compare to samples I've got, but I can't run 'em through the database. You want me to send them to Tallahassee?"

"Yes, please," she answered. "Do me a favor; call Steve Pruitt. Tell him it's for me and beg him to rush it."

"I'll try," he said. "Talk to you when I know something."

Maggie hung up and chewed at her lower lip. Even with special attention, it could take three or four days to hear back, maybe more. But if she could conceivably place someone else on the dock with Marisol, smoking her cigarettes, then it helped Axel, even if the person in question was an unknown.

She dumped her empty coffee cup into the trash can beside her desk, grabbed her purse from a drawer, and headed out.

CHAPTER

SEVENTEEN

When her cell phone rang, Maggie was coming out of Piggly Wiggly with ingredients for a dinner that made her feel like a bad mother. She transferred one of the two bags to her other hand and dug her phone out of her purse.

"Hey, Dwight," she said as she walked to her Jeep.

"Hey, Maggie," he replied, sounding excited. "Guess who just returned my crap-ton of calls?"

"Who?"

"Gavin Betancourt. Says he just got back from the Exumas, and he can meet with us tomorrow," Dwight said. "I told him we'd come down to Tampa in the morning. Right?"

"Yeah," she answered. She pinned her phone to her shoulder with her chin, and opened the back door. "How'd he sound?"

"Like he was too good for me," Dwight said.

"Awesome." Maggie put the bags on the back seat and leaned on the door. She got the feeling for a second that someone was looking at her, and turned around expecting to see a friend or neighbor walking up behind her, but there was no one there. She realized Dwight was still talking.

"I'm sorry, what?"

"I said they got 7-11s down there," Dwight answered. "Reckon we can stop and get me one of those white mocha coffee things?"

"Oh, Dwight," Maggie said, sighing. "You're making me sick. Let me bring you something from Apalachicola Coffee."

"Uh, thanks, but no," he said. "That time I drank your spare I was up for two days and I couldn't feel my brain."

"Okay, suit yourself," Maggie said. "I've got to get home to the kids. I'll see you first thing."

"Okee-doke."

She disconnected the call and shut the back door, then stood there and looked around the small parking lot. A young blonde woman was at the end of Maggie's row, putting a huge bag of dog food into the back of her minivan. In the middle of the only other row, an elderly man Maggie knew only by sight was closing his door and heading inside. Neither of them paid her any attention, but she still felt attention was being paid.

She looked out at the street, but saw no one. The parking lot of the tiny police station across the street was empty. Maggie took a slower pass over the cars parked at Piggly Wiggly, but saw no one sitting in their cars. She waited a moment, then climbed into the driver's seat and started the Cherokee.

One block away, at the CVS across the street, a lit cigarette was flicked out of an open window. Its embers bounced, looking like tiny fireworks in the dusk, then died before another engine started.

⚓ ⚓ ⚓

The drive from Apalach to Tampa was not one of Maggie's favorites. Every cell in her body was Floridian, but she was from a Florida that didn't exist outside the Panhandle, and she had no use for most of the rest of the state.

The drive was 98 almost all the way, until it turned into Suncoast Pkwy down around Crystal River. Maggie didn't mind 98; it was largely woods, with a few quick passes through a few Podunk towns, but Maggie was partial to Podunk. Once they got onto the Parkway, though, they were dumped into a touristy Florida from the 1950s. Even that was better than what greeted them once they hit Tampa about an hour later; nothing but high-rises, strip malls, real malls, and slums. As far as Maggie was concerned, Jacksonville, Miami, Tampa, Orlando, they were all the same, except that Orlando put on a nice front.

Gavin Betancourt didn't exactly live in Tampa proper; his home was located in Davis Islands, a small island in the Tampa Bay that was connected to mainland Tampa by a short bridge. It was an area of seriously overpriced Spanish style and ultra-modern homes. Maggie loathed it on sight. She didn't mind wealth, she just preferred it to have a little restraint.

Betancourt's home was of the modern variety, a coral-colored two story house on Adalia, which would mean that his back yard was the bay itself. Maggie pulled into the circular gravel drive and felt like she ought to apologize to her car for letting it show up looking like that.

Dwight blew out a breath. "I get surprised every now and then by how well dealing drugs pays," he said.

"Yeah," Maggie said. "There's a real future in it, if you ever get tired of sleeping at night."

"Ah, that's okay," Dwight said. "If I was rich, I'd have to hang out with rich people, and I don't like 'em much."

He and Maggie got out of the Cherokee, and were halfway to the carved, double front door when one side of it opened.

"Lt. Redmond?" the man standing there asked.

He was in his late forties, Maggie guessed, with blond hair that brushed against the collar of his green silk shirt. He wasn't a handsome man, but he was striking. Her overall impression was that he looked expensive.

He waited with a half-smile, as Maggie and Dwight made their way to the terracotta steps.

"Mr. Betancourt?" Maggie asked.

"That would be me, yes." He didn't extend a hand. Maggie was okay with that.

"I'm Lt. Redmond and this is Deputy Shultz," Maggie said politely. "Thank you for seeing us."

"I had options?" he asked with a smirk.

"You have good lawyers, I'm sure," Maggie responded.

"I do," he answered, as he held the door open wider and stepped back to let them in. "But I also have nothing to cause me to avoid you."

Maggie and Dwight stepped into a two-story entryway that was flooded with sunlight from two skylights and a wall of windows in the room beyond the circular staircase. Betancourt preceded them down the hall toward the back, waving them to follow, like good little strays.

"Let's talk back here," he said, as he led them into a room that looked like it ran across the entire rear of the house. The windows that made up the back wall looked out onto the bay, and to the two boats that were tied up at his private dock. One was a speedboat Maggie didn't recognize. The other was a circa 1990's Tollycraft Pilothouse that had to be fifty feet long. Maggie could retire on the proceeds of selling it.

"Is that the boat you took to the Exumas?" she asked Betancourt as they crossed to an arrangement of Danish modern chairs and couches.

"Yes, it is," Betancourt answered. "Do you know Tolly-crafts?"

"Not personally," she answered as she sat in a turquoise chair that wasn't half as comfortable as one wanted it to be.

Dwight perched on the edge of a matching chair, and Betancourt slid down onto a loveseat that faced them. Between them was an angular glass coffee table that reflected enough sunlight to make Maggie squint.

"Can I get either of you some coffee, something cold?" Betancourt asked.

"No, thank you," Maggie answered politely. Dwight shook his head. "We'll try not to take too much of your time."

Betancourt sighed and leaned forward, resting his elbows on his knees. "I was sorry to hear about Marisol," he said quietly, but without emotion. "but I'm not sure how I can help you."

"We're speaking with anyone who knew her well," Maggie replied. "You were together for a while, weren't you?"

"Yes, for about a year," Betancourt answered.

"When did you split?"

He looked up at the ceiling as though trying to remember, but given the reason for their visit, Maggie knew he didn't need to. "The first part of April, I think.

"Why?"

"Nothing in particular," he answered. "My interest cooled. Marisol was a lovely woman, but we didn't have very much in common."

"Did you love her?"

He smiled in a way that was meant to look apologetic, but wasn't. "No. I enjoyed her company. She was very vibrant, she could be a lot of fun. But nothing like love, no."

"Did she leave you for Toby Mann?"

"She didn't leave me at all," he answered. "She ran straight from me to him, but I was the one who ended our relationship."

"Do you know Toby?" Maggie asked.

"Sure. He used to work for me."

"What did he do?"

"Marketing," Betancourt answered with a quick smile. Maggie had seen barracudas smile with more warmth.

"When did he stop working for you?"

"A year or so ago," he replied. "It was amicable. I was relieved to see him go, actually."

"Why is that?"

Betancourt sighed just a little. "He wasn't as bright as his arrogance suggested."

Maggie chewed the corner of her lip for a moment. "Mr. Betancourt, I'm not especially interested in your business dealings. My concern is Franklin County, not Tampa. So I hope you'll speak frankly with me."

"I have nothing to hide, Lieutenant." Again, that insincere smile.

"Toby Mann says he didn't know Marisol was in Apalachicola," Maggie said. "But she told someone that she was there on her boyfriend's behalf. On behalf of his business."

Betancourt fashioned his expression into something approaching regretful, then leaned back against the cushions of the loveseat. "Well, that's a little sad."

"That she was trying to help him build his, uh, business?"

He waited a moment before answering. "No, that she referred to me as her boyfriend."

That took Maggie a second. "She was there for you?"

"No, not exactly," he said, leaning forward again. "Bear in mind, please, that I'm no longer in the business that gained me some notoriety with local law enforcement."

"Wow," Dwight popped up quietly. "All the drug dealers we talk to are retired."

Betancourt threw him an irritated smile, then looked back at Maggie. "In any case, back when I might have dabbled a bit, my clientele, and my products, were of a more sophisticated quality."

"More sophisticated than what?"

"Than what Toby Mann was targeting," he answered. "You're familiar with gravel, I'm sure."

Maggie nodded. Gravel, or flakka, was a problem that was growing exponentially. It was dirt cheap; a person could get high for hours on five dollars, but it was also extremely dangerous and very addicting. The benefit to Florida dealers was that it cost so little, was available from China or Pakistan in huge quantities, and was relatively easy to transport. Gravel dealers targeted the poor and working class, because they could afford to get hooked.

"Toby had his sights set on becoming some big-time gravel distributor," Betancourt went on. "It was cheap enough to buy quite large quantities. Within his limited budget."

"What does that have to do with you?"

"Not much at all," Betancourt said. "Except that Marisol told me that Toby was trying to set up transportation systems, get in with legitimate businesses that had such systems, trucking and so on, and use them to distribute to associates in north Florida, where he thought the market was good for a cheap high."

Maggie had spent some time in narcotics. She had to admit that Toby was right. North Florida was full of the poor, the working class, and students on tight budgets. "She told you that why?"

"She was trying to sell me the idea."

"Why would she do that, Mr. Betancourt? It seems like she'd be shooting herself in the foot."

"She wanted away from Toby," he answered. "And she was hoping we could get back together. I think she thought she could accomplish that by helping me implement Toby's idea."

Maggie stared out at the perfectly manicured grass between the house and the dock. Boudreaux had a fleet of boats, as well as a trucking company that transported produce and seafood throughout the south. Marisol would have known about Boudreaux from her time in Apalach with Axel. She probably wouldn't have known about his disdain for drugs, though. She looked back at Betancourt.

"Why did she want to end her relationship with Toby?"

"Marisol outclassed Toby by a wide margin. I'm sure she realized that pretty quickly," he answered. "But he was also very volatile."

"Abusive volatile?"

"Yes."

"That's odd," she replied. "He told us that you used to beat Marisol."

"Did he now?" His voice had grown chilly, but he still appeared relaxed enough. "I don't raise my hand to women."

"How do you know he did?"

"Marisol told me," Betancourt answered. "I think she was hoping I'd avenge her, get her out, take care of her problem."

Maggie looked at him a moment. "Why didn't you?"

He held her gaze for a moment, then held up his hands. "It wasn't my business."

"She was your girlfriend at one time."

"At one time," he replied. "I wished her well, but I'm no one's knight in shining armor."

Maggie didn't doubt the truth of that. "When was the last time you talked to her?"

He didn't bother pretending to think it over. "Tuesday morning. She said she was on her way to talk to someone that she thought might be interested in her proposal, whatever that was."

"So she was in Apalach when you last spoke?"

"Yes. She liked it up there, you know. Had ties there. I think she was thinking about relocating."

Maggie sighed. She had the sense of Marisol flailing for some kind of peace, and even though she'd never really liked Mari, she was sad for her. She sat forward as something occurred to her. "Do you remember the number she called you from?"

Betancourt frowned at her. "No, but I remember that I didn't recognize it. I think she got a new phone." He raised his body to reach into his back pocket, and removed a new Galaxy from it. He thumbed through it for a moment, then held a page of recent calls up for her to see. "That 813 number was her call," he said. Maggie recognized it as the phone they'd found in her room.

"But you know another number for her?"

"Yes." He tapped on his contacts list, thumbed it a moment, then showed her a listing for Mari.

Maggie didn't recognize the number. She jotted it down. "Do you remember the last time she called you from that number?"

"It was right before she left for your area," he answered. "The day before, I think. I can look it up."

"That's okay," she said.

"I have a lunch appointment at noon," he said. "Do you need anything else?"

Maggie stood, and Dwight stood with her, trying not to look enthusiastic about leaving. "No, not at the moment," Maggie said. "Thank you for your time."

⚓ ⚓ ⚓

Maggie turned on the Jeep and rolled down the front windows, letting in air that felt cleaner than the air had been inside the big, fancy house. After a moment, Dwight looked over at her, his Adam's apple bobbing like a hungry baby bird.

"You know, it really kinks my hose that these big-time drug dealers have money they don't even know about, and honest people have to choose between paying the electric bill and the water," he said.

"Yeah," Maggie said, nodding distractedly. She stared out the windshield at a small waterfall in the middle of Betancourt's landscaping. "I think he's telling the truth about why Marisol was in Apalach. She wasn't there for

Toby Mann. And I think Toby knew she was up there, and what she was doing."

"You think he just knew about Axel, or that she was trying to take his idea and hand it to this guy.?"

"I don't know," she answered. "But he doesn't seem like the kind of guy who would take the business thing too lightly, especially if he was violent."

"You know, I wouldn't be surprised if Betancourt told him," Dwight said. "Honor among drug dealers or some kinda thing like that."

"Maybe," she answered, then sighed. "Geez."

"What's wrong?"

"It's just so damn sad." She looked over at Dwight. "We've got two suspects besides Axel, and both of them are saying they just didn't care enough about Marisol to have killed her."

Dwight nodded. "Yeah, that's pretty crappy," he said. "Such a beautiful woman, but nobody cared about her."

"Axel did," Maggie said quietly.

Dwight was quiet for a moment. "Yeah, it's a shame about that."

CHAPTER
EIGHTEEN

Maggie and Dwight got back to Franklin County around four. Maggie had been slightly lead-footed, and they both breathed better once they hit Sopchoppy, like the air was easier to inhale on home ground. Maggie was frequently conflicted; she'd love a vacation, but she didn't actually like leaving Apalach.

Maggie dropped Dwight off to get his car at the Sheriff's Office, and she headed across the bridge to Apalach. Once she was on the Gorrie, she glanced over at the riverfront, as she always did. She could just make out the Water Street Hotel and Marina at the end, and she amended her plans just a bit.

Water Street was a nice place, a neat, three-story place that only had thirty units, several of them actually condos. It sat right on the creek, and had several slips for rent at its own docks. It was quiet and clean, each unit had two bedrooms, a full kitchen, and a screened in balcony overlooking the creek. Lucky guests also got a free temporary cat, one of the three that had taken up permanent residence. If Maggie needed a place to stay, she would stay at Water Street.

She pulled up to the hotel, got out, and gratefully stretched her legs and butt for a minute before heading across the parking lot to the front office.

When she walked in, the night clerk, Linda, looked up from her computer. Maggie and Linda knew each other from softball and high school functions, and Maggie was rather fond of the other woman. She was black, with hair cut as short as it could be without being gone. She was in her forties, nicely plump, and wore her reading glasses on her nose and her regular glasses on her head. Both of them reflected the light from the ceiling fan when she looked up at Maggie.

"Hey, girl, how you been?" she asked with a big smile full of beautiful white teeth.

Maggie walked up to the chest-high wooden counter. "Good, Linda. How are you?"

"Oh, you know," Linda answered. "Same old things. I haven't seen you in ages. We need to meet up at Papa Joe's one of these days, have some lunch."

"That would be great," Maggie said, and she meant it. Her world was getting smaller and less populated all the time, and the only woman she saw regularly was her mother.

"Hold up while I finish this real quick." Linda said as she tapped a couple of keys. "What are you doing over here?"

"I came over here to talk to one of your guests, but I didn't see his car, so I thought I'd talk to you instead."

"Oh, girl, please," Linda said. "I don't have the time or energy for any kinda crime over in here. What'd he do?"

"Probably nothing," Maggie lied.

"Hold on, it's time for me to smoke," Linda said, getting up from her chair. She grabbed a pack of cigarettes and a lighter from a desk drawer, and came out of the office, opened the glass door to the docks. Maggie followed her out, and waited while she lit her cigarette and blew out her first drag.

"Is it the old man with the sunspots on his head?" Linda asked, a hand on her hip. "He keeps undressing me with his eyes, not that he doesn't have good reason."

Maggie smiled. "No, a young guy. Toby Mann, from Tampa."

"Oh, him," Linda replied, sounding bored already. "What about him?"

"Peggy from day shift said he checked in on Saturday?"

"Yeah, that sounds right," Linda answered. "What's wrong with him?"

Maggie shook her head, though that meant nothing. "What do you think about him?"

"Honey, I don't have an opinion on the man, outside the fact he seems to think he's a whole lot better looking than he actually is," Linda answered. "He came down one night asking me where's the closest liquor store. Seemed like he thought I should be all excited he was standing there. I don't think I've seen him three times since then, but we close the office at eleven. He's probably still out then."

"Do you remember seeing anyone here with him?" Maggie asked.

"Nope, don't think so." Linda blew a mouthful of smoke over the aluminum rail. "I don't think he hangs out here too much, though."

"Why's that?"

"Janie says there's almost nothing to do when she goes to clean the room," Linda answered. "She mentioned it yesterday, said she didn't even need to make the bed. I guess he found somewhere else to sleep, you know what I mean?"

Maggie thought about that a minute. "When's the last time you saw him?"

"Let me think," Linda said. "Day before yesterday? When I came in to work. He's not checked out, though. I got a note he's staying a few more days or so."

Maggie nodded. "Okay." Mann was supposed to be a stranger here. So where was he spending his time?

"I need to be scared of this guy?" Linda asked her, glaring down her nose at her.

"No, not at all, Linda," Maggie said. "His girlfriend is the woman they found over at Riverview Thursday morning."

"Huh," the other woman huffed. She took another drag of her cigarette. "Well, I don't think he's mourning much."

⚓ ⚓ ⚓

After a long day of driving outside her comfort zone, Maggie needed some refueling. She came out of Apalachicola Coffee, took a long swallow of freshly-roasted Guatemalan Antigua, and surveyed Market Street. Apalach virtually closed down by 9pm, but it was generally hopping at cocktail and dinner time, and today was no exception.

At the corner, two doors down, customers sat at the black iron tables outside Tamara's, laughing and sipping their beer or wine. Diagonally across the street, the Seafood Grill was doing a brisk early dinner business, and a few doors down on her right, customers were streaming out of The Soda Fountain carrying ice creams, shark tooth necklaces, and postcards. Seeing the ice cream made Maggie miss Wyatt. It also made her miss the days when Axel's biggest problem was whether they—Maggie, David and Axel—had enough money between them to get a banana split.

She looked away from the family sitting at the picnic table outside the shop, and her gaze jerked to a stop on the sidewalk across the street. There was a blue Elantra parked across the street from Tamara's, and Toby Mann was leaning against his open door, smoking a cigarette. It occurred to Maggie to wonder if he'd been following her, if he was the reason she kept feeling ants crawling on the back of her neck.

He was watching the people on the sidewalk, and didn't notice her until she was halfway across the street. He tossed his cigarette butt on the ground and nodded at her.

"Hello, Lieutenant," he said.

"Hello, Mr. Mann," she answered. "Going in for dinner?"

"No, I just stopped in for a beer," he said, then raised his hands. "Just one."

"Relax, Mr. Mann," she said pleasantly. "I know there's not much to do here for someone who's used to the city."

"Well, I didn't come for entertainment," he said.

"I stopped by Water Street earlier," Maggie said.

"You have some news?" he asked, looking hopeful.

"No, I wanted to ask you if you knew where Marisol's iPhone is," Maggie answered, taking a sip of her coffee.

"No," he replied. "I figured you people had it."

"No, we haven't found it." Maggie pulled out her own phone.

"Well, I don't know," he said, as Maggie tapped through her screens. "Maybe the river?"

"Maybe," Maggie answered as she tapped on Marisol's number, which she'd transferred to her contacts list.

She was hoping it would ring. In fact, she was hoping she'd hear it ringing through Toby's pants pocket or the open window of his car, but it went straight to voice mail. She felt Toby waiting, and she hung up and glanced at him. "The battery's probably dead," she said. "or it's turned off."

"Probably dead," he said. "She was bad about charging it."

"Since she's on your plan, you can track her phone, can't you? she asked. "Can you check it?"

"It won't work if the phone's off," Toby said, his eyes darting over her shoulder at nothing much.

Maggie nodded. "That's too bad," she said. "Most likely, you're right though. If Marisol was like me, she kept her phone on her pretty much all the time. It's most likely in Scipio Creek."

"Is it important?" Mann asked her.

"No, not really," she said. "Just a loose end."

"What about her ex-husband? You still working on him?" Toby's eyes narrowed as he asked.

"Right now, that's pretty much all we do have to work on," she answered. "But I'll let you know if there are any developments." That wasn't true, but saying it served its purpose.

"Well, okay," he said. He turned and slid into his car. "I'll be waiting."

Maggie watched him pull out and drive away, toward 98. She watched him turn right, then she committed the plate to memory, and bent down to pick up his cigarette butt. Then she walked back across the street to her Jeep. She opened the gate of the Cherokee and flipped the lid on the red toolbox she used as a crime scene kit.

Down the block, in front of the bank, a truck engine started, then pulled into the light traffic.

Maggie was digging an evidence bag out of her kit when Axel passed by in a borrowed Ford F-150. He glanced at the back of Maggie, then turned right after Toby Mann.

⚓ ⚓ ⚓

Maggie climbed into the driver's seat and shut her door, then glanced at her old Timex. 5:40. The lab closed at 5pm. She went through her contacts and called Mike on his cell.

"Yo," he answered.

"Hey, Mike," Maggie said. "Listen, first thing in the morning, I need you to compare a cigarette butt I just acquired with the results from the unknown butts on the dock."

"I can do that," he said.

The Sheriff's Office didn't have the facilities to run DNA, but simple blood and saliva tests could tell them if they had a likely match between one sample and another.

The blood type and analysis on the first butts would be in the computer file on the case.

"You didn't hear anything back yet from Tallahassee, did you?' Maggie asked, though she knew it was seriously unlikely.

"Maggie," Mike said reproachfully.

"I know. Just thought I'd ask."

"But I can find out if we're on the right track," he said.

"Okay, I'll see you bright and early," Maggie said, and hung up. She turned on the ignition before dialing Dwight.

"Hey, Dwight," she said when he answered. "I got the rest of the plate number on Mann's rental car."

"Shoot," Dwight said, and she heard him scrambling for something to write with. In the background, she could hear one of his kids laughing. He had three, all under the age of seven.

"453-BVN" Maggie recited. "Can you call and have somebody run it?"

"Yeah, but it might be morning before we hear back, so you might as well let me do it," Dwight said. "Some of those places were giving me the runaround on account of we don't have a warrant or anything. I been having to go through the manager types, and those guys aren't around at night."

Maggie sighed. "Okay. Morning, then. I'll see you tomorrow. Go play with your kids."

"Angel's teaching me how to Dab."

"What's that?"

"I don't know," he said. "Reckon that's why she's teaching me."

Maggie hung up and stared out her windshield at a Dalmation that nobody owned and everybody fed. He was ambling down the sidewalk toward the dog fountain in front of the ice cream place.

Dwight was a great father. It was one of the things she liked most about him. He sheltered his kids, but he didn't lie to them much. Like many law enforcement officers, he told his kids the truth about the world in as few words and as little detail as he could, but he told the truth nonetheless. Daddy had done the same, with the exception of Bennett Boudreaux being her biological father.

She sighed, put the Jeep in reverse, and started home.

CHAPTER
NINETEEN

When Maggie got to the office just after 7:30, she bypassed her own office and walked straight to the lab. Mike was at his desk, drinking from an enormous travel mug emblazoned with a Crimson Tide logo.

"Hey, Maggie," he said, smiling.

Maggie reached into her purse and yanked out the evidence bag as she hurried over to Mike. "Hey, Mike."

"This your butt?' he asked as she held it out to him.

"Yeah," she answered as he read the label to make sure she'd filled it out properly. "How soon can you get it back to me?"

"Pretty soon," he answered. "I have to finish something else up, then you're next in line."

"Okay." Maggie started for the door. "Call me on my cell, okay?"

"Will do," he said to her back.

She walked to her office down the hall, passing Wyatt's office as she went. He wasn't in yet. She remembered him saying something about coming in late that morning since he'd worked late earlier in the week.

She dropped her purse into her desk drawer and sat down to answer messages.

An hour later, Dwight popped into her doorway, his Adam's apple bobbing more enthusiastically than usual. "Uh, hey, Maggie? We got the rental car." He walked over to her desk, a piece of scrap paper in his hand. "He rented it from Enterprise in Panama City on Friday."

Maggie sat back a second. "Friday." Mann had said he'd gotten there Saturday. "Panama City. He flew in?"

"Nope, I checked that already, when we first saw he was driving a rental. More interesting than that," Dwight answered. "Did you know Enterprise will bring your rental car to you?"

"Yeah? So where'd they take his car?"

"Best Western out on 98," Dwight said, looking happy.

Maggie frowned up at him. "Why? Call Best Western and asked if he was registered there."

"Reckon I done it already," Dwight said. "He wasn't staying there."

"What the hell," Maggie said quietly.

"Kinda my thought, too," Dwight said. "But they dropped the car off to him at 4:20pm on Friday. He was here a day before he said he was, and he had to be staying somewhere. But he wasn't at the Best Western."

He plopped his hands onto the place his hips would have been, if he'd had some. "Gets interesting from there, too. He had Enterprise come get the car last night."

"At Best Western?"

"Nope. Water Street. They took it a little after five."

That would have been shortly after Maggie had seen him on Market Street. She flicked through some Post-it notes on her desk, found the number she was looking for, picked up her desk phone, and dialed. Peggy answered on the second ring.

"Water Street Hotel and Marina, this is Peggy speaking. How can I help you?"

"Hey, Peggy, this is Maggie Redmond," Maggie said in a rush. "Has Toby Mann checked out?"

"I don't think so, but check out time isn't till eleven," Peggy answered. "Hold on."

Maggie listened for a moment as Peggy tapped at her keyboard.

"Nope, he hasn't checked out or anything," Peggy said. "And I know he was here last night, because there's a note here that he needed a new room key. His got magnetized."

"I need you to do me a favor," Maggie said. "Can you call his room phone, see if he's there?"

"What do I say?"

"Just ask him if he needs housekeeping or towels or something," Maggie answered. "I just need to know if he's actually still there."

"Okay," Peggy said, sounding fairly reluctant. "Hold on a sec."

Maggie glanced up at Dwight as Peggy put her on hold. She listened to a recording about the hotel's winter rates as she chewed the corner of her lip. Peggy came back on about a minute later.

"Maggie? He's there. He was kind of mad."

"Okay, Peggy," Maggie said. "Thanks, I appreciate it."

She hung up the phone, then sat forward and drummed the fingers of both hands against her desk as she stared at the fake wood grain. Dwight waited.

"So, he just magically appears in town on Friday. Why didn't he just drive his own car up here?" Maggie asked the desk. "And why didn't he check into Water Street until Saturday?"

"It's a perplexment for sure," Dwight said. "I was thinking maybe somebody dropped him off up here. What do you think?"

Maggie frowned at the air for a moment. "Possibility, but it doesn't make much sense," she said. "Of course, this guy's like a garter snake; he's sneaking around doing all kinds of crap that I don't get. I was thinking before you came in. We've been thinking Mari used this other phone of hers because she didn't want Mann tracking her here, but the phone wasn't a secret. We got his phone number from her recent calls."

"Huh. Yeah," Dwight said.

"Maybe she had the second phone for business they didn't want traced to their iPhone accounts."

"Sounds logical."

She rapped on her desk a few times. "Do me a favor; run over to Water Street and just sit on the place. If he goes anywhere, you go with him. Take your car, though. No cruiser. I'm going to take another look at her phone."

"Got it," Dwight said, and hustled out of the office.

⚓ ⚓ ⚓

A few minutes later, Maggie had retrieved the cell phone from evidence, plugged it in, and powered it up. She scrolled through the contacts list again. The last call from this phone had been on Tuesday night. It was to Axel, which meant little to Maggie, and nothing else she found in the contacts did, either. They'd traced every call on the list, though there weren't many. She tapped the screen to go back to the home screen, and was about to shut it off when one of the icons caught her eye. The icon meant little, a blue and silver-striped sphere. But when she tapped it, it turned out to be an app for Barclay bank. Mann had never said which credit card he'd gotten for Mari, but Maggie knew her secured card was from Credit One.

She stared at the app's open page, which was asking her to log in. The user name was filled in. It was Mari80. Marisol had been born in 1980, Maggie knew. She stared at the space for the password a moment, then tried

Mari80. She wasn't surprised when it came back invalid. She considered for a moment, then typed in Axel78. Invalid. She sucked in a breath. She knew that the app would probably lock her out after one or two more tries.

She stared at it for a moment, then picked up her own cell phone.

"Hey, Maggie," Axel answered after the first ring.

"Hey, Axel," Maggie said. "What year did you and Marisol get married?"

"The first or second time?"

"Both."

"The first time was 1991," he answered. "The second time was...'99. Why?"

"I'll tell you later," she said. "How are you?"

"I'm okay." He didn't even sound like he was trying to convince himself.

"What are you doing?"

"Having coffee at the house with Wyatt," he answered.

"With—Wyatt doesn't drink Maxwell House," she said stupidly.

"He brought his own," Axel said.

"Ok, well, I've got to go. I'll talk to you later, okay?"

"Okay, see you later."

Maggie hung up, then picked up Marisol's phone, stared at the app as she sent up a silent prayer, then typed in Axel91. When the app opened up, she let out a breath she hadn't known she was holding.

The last day the card showed transactions was two days before. Tamara's. Maggie hadn't realized that charges from both Mari's and Mann's cards would be on the same account, but she guessed that made sense, since Mari was only an authorized user. Over the previous few days, there were miscellaneous, uninteresting charges from local restaurants and gas stations. Friday was more interesting, with a charge from Enterprise of Panama City, made that morning. Nothing for Thursday, the day they'd found Marisol's body.

But Wednesday afternoon, there was a charge for almost $400 in Tampa. It was from Bayside Marine Fueling Center.

⚓ ⚓ ⚓

Wyatt watched as Axel hung up the phone, then took another sip of coffee from a chipped mug. He'd come over to Axel's small house on 4th Street to check up on him, see how he was holding up. He'd been expecting the man to be drunk or asleep, but he was neither. Axel was on his second pot of coffee, and Wyatt had joined him on his covered back patio, where the ceiling full of old buoys and the homemade hammock, made out of shrimp netting, achieved an authenticity that nautical-minded decorators would never manage.

"What's up with Maggie?" Wyatt asked him.

"I don't know man," Axel answered. "She wanted to know when Mari and I got married."

Wyatt nodded, stared out at the back yard, where a small fountain was encircled by antique glass buoys in various colors.

"Let me ask you something, Axel," Wyatt said finally.

"No, we never dated," Axel said.

"What?"

Axel looked over at him. "Maggie and I never went out," he said simply.

"I know that," Wyatt said, irritation tinting his voice.

"Oh. Well, then what?"

"Why the heck did you get yourself a shrimp boat instead of going to MIT?"

Axel stretched out his legs and propped his bare feet on an old gear box. "I didn't. My dad left me the boat," he said.

"Don't be an asspain," Wyatt said. "Why didn't you go?"

Axel shrugged. "I can understand and prove Fermat's last theorem, but that doesn't mean I give a gnat's ass about it."

"Fermat," Wyatt said. "Is he a local?"

Axel was going to say something snarky, but Wyatt's grin told him he knew Fermat didn't live in Apalach. "I guess we won't go into the applications of elliptic curves and crap," he said instead.

"I appreciate that," Wyatt said. He took a long drink of his coffee, then shrugged after he'd swallowed. "Hey, at least you're pretty good at totaling up the night's catch, huh?"

"Not without sticking my tongue out, man," Axel answered.

Wyatt touched his ball cap in appreciation, then unfurled himself from the too-low for his height Adirondack chair. "I gotta get going."

Axel got up, too, and stretched his legs. "Me, too. I've got some work to do on the boat."

"Lucky you. My new fearless leader has me talking to the Chamber of Commerce today about some kind of tourist safety crap."

"I give it two months before you shoot him and take your job back, man," he said.

"That's way too optimistic," Wyatt replied.

CHAPTER
TWENTY

aggie had left two messages, on what she was pretty sure was an actual answering machine, for the dockmaster at Bayside Marina in Tampa. So far, she hadn't heard back, and her admittedly low patience had spun out already.

She killed time checking on Dwight's surveillance of Water Street, which was uneventful thus far, and by reading up on gravel, or flakka. South Florida was having a heck of a time with it, particularly with the gruesome side effects the drug had on many people.

One man had tried to eat the face of another in a Publix parking lot in Dania. A teenaged girl had accidentally impaled herself on a fence in Hollywood, while she was running away from demons. A man in Fort Lauderdale had been caught trying to have sex with a tree at Holiday Park in Fort Lauderdale. Maggie wasn't sure how that was supposed to work, but she was sure of one thing: she didn't want this crap anywhere near Franklin County. The more she read, the less sorry she felt for the sad, dead woman who had once eaten dinner in her home.

Maggie told Google to leave her alone, then drummed her fingers on her desk for a moment before grabbing the case file, rifling through the pages from Tampa PD, and then picking up her cell phone to make a call.

"Sgt. Freeman," a deep voice answered. It had a touch of the northeast to it.

"Sergeant, this is Lt. Maggie Redmond from the Franklin County Sheriff's Office," Maggie said. "You sent us some info a few days ago on a man named Toby Mann."

"Tobias Mann, yeah, he's a popular guy this week," the man said. "He's a real winner."

"I've been trying to get in touch with the dockmaster at Bayside Marina down there," Maggie said. "Do you know if Mann has a boat?"

"Yeah, he's got a boat," Freeman answered. "Makes a big deal about it, thinks he's Scarface or somebody, you know, not the run of the mill dumbass that he is."

"Do you know what kind of boat?"

"No, not a clue. I'm from Pennsylvania, you know? But it's a nice one." Maggie heard him fumble with the phone, maybe switching ears. "You know who you need to talk to, though, is Det. Bruce. We were just talking about Mann this morning."

"What about?" Maggie asked.

"Hold on, let me let you talk to him, right?"

Maggie sat through an eternity of seconds on hold until someone else picked up the line.

"Lt. Redmond?"

"Yeah," Maggie said, sitting up.

"Ryan Bruce, narcotics. Larry said you're asking about Toby Mann?"

"Yeah, I am. I was calling to find out if he has a boat."

"Yeah, I saw where you people requested his file a few days ago," Bruce said. "I was planning on giving you folks a call later."

"What's up?"

"Well, to answer your first question, yeah he has a boat," Bruce said. "He does a lot of partying on it, entertaining clients and so forth, acting like a big man. But he also likes to meet with people out on the water. Either he thinks it's more private, or he thinks it's more impressive."

"Do you know what kind of boat it is?" Maggie asked.

"No, not offhand, but I can find out," Bruce answered. "But the reason I was going to give you a call is that we got a heads up from an informant this morning. Said Mann's supposed to be meeting up with some guys from up around Panama City."

"What kind of guys?" Maggie asked.

"Guys we don't like," Bruce answered. "Our informant says they were originally supposed to be meeting with someone else, out on the water, like Mann likes to do, back on Thursday night, but that got cancelled. Now we hear it's back on, per Toby Mann."

"Where?"

"We don't have a time or coordinates yet. We've been in touch with the Coast Guard up your way, so we can try to get some names for these people from their boat registration, but we can't really do anything other than gather information," Bruce explained. "This is just a meet and greet, a first date. No product, no money."

"Your informant works for Mann?"

"No, he works for a guy Mann used to work for."

"Gavin Betancourt?"

"Yeah, you know him?"

"We've met, "Maggie answered. "So how would Gavin's guy know about this meeting?"

"Apparently, Betancourt's the one that told Mann about the original meeting," Bruce answered. "But Mann's the one that cancelled it, and he's the one rescheduled it."

Maggie stared at the old Café Bustelo can she used to hold her pens. Betancourt had set Mari up. He'd either set her up, or sold her out, by telling Toby about the meeting. He might as well have had his hands around her neck, too.

"Anyhow, I can update you if anything comes of this thing tonight, but that's what I got," Bruce said. "You want me to get a car to run by the marina and see what kind of boat Mann's got?"

"Yeah, if you don't mind," Maggie said distractedly. "I'm on my way to go talk to him."

"You're working the thing with his girlfriend, right?"

"Yeah."

"Well, tell him we said 'Hi', would you?"

"Sure thing," Maggie answered as she got up from her desk, automatically touching the .45 in her holster.

"I'll be in touch."

He hung up and Maggie grabbed her purse and phone and hurried out of her office.

⚓ ⚓ ⚓

Maggie's phone rang as she pulled out of the Sheriff's Office parking lot. She thought of a few bad words when she saw that she only had about three-percent left on her battery. She'd loaned Sky her car charger the night before and forgotten to get it back. She thumbed open the call.

"Hello?"

"Is this Lieutenant Redmond?" asked an older male voice she didn't recognize.

"Yes, it is."

"This is Paul Hammer, from Bayside Marine? I just got your message, ma'am."

"Yes, thank you for getting back to me," Maggie said as she turned left onto 65.

"You were wanting to know about Mr. Mann's boat?"

"Yes, sir," Maggie answered.

"Well, it's a nice 'un. '85 Bertram, the Mark 3," he said. "But we've never had no trouble here with him."

Maggie headed him off at the pass. "There's nothing for you to worry about, Mr. Hammer," she said. "I just need to know about the boat. Is it there?"

"Well, no," he said, sounding relieved that it wasn't. "He pulled out...oh, it was Wednesday. I don't recall what time exactly, but it was after lunch and before I left for the dentist at four."

"Did he say where he was going?"

"Nope, but he filled her up earlier in the day," he said. "She's got the twin Cats, you know. 375s. He had 'em put in last year. She'll move for ya, but she'll guzzle some diesel while she's doing it."

"Mr. Hammer, do you have the name and registration number for her?" Maggie asked, pulling over to the side of the road.

"Yes, ma'am, I pulled 'em for ya."

Maggie grabbed a pen from the console and wrote the information down on the back of some mail. "Thank you, sir. I appreciate you getting back to me."

She heard him start to say something, but she disconnected anyway. She thumbed open her contacts list and tapped the most logical name there before she pulled back out onto the road.

Her father answered on the first ring. "Hey, Sunshine," he said in his gentle voice.

"Hey, Daddy," she said hurriedly. "Listen, I just have a second, my phone's about to die. I have a question."

"Okay."

"A Bertram Mark 3. How fast could it get here from Tampa?"

"Well, let's see. If she's got the single screw, she's not going to be a speed demon—"

"It's got twin Cats," Maggie interrupted. "375s."

"Well now," Gray said, sounding impressed. "That's different. I'd say she'll do 25-30 knots if you're pushing her, but you're gonna have to stop for fuel along the way at those speeds. I don't recall for sure, but I'd say that boat'll hold 300 gallons or so. If you're pushing it, you got maybe six hours of fuel for a seven, eight hour trip. So I'd say maybe eight, nine hours, with refueling."

Maggie tried to do math in her head. Toby was at his restaurant opening at least until three, but no one swore they saw him after that. If he left the marina as late as four, that meant he'd get to Apalach around midnight or one.

"She's a nice vessel, Sunshine, but she's got no style," her father was saying. "She's no Grand Banks."

"I'm not shopping, Daddy, I'm working," she said. "I appreciate it."

"Anyti—"

Maggie's phone went dead, and she dropped it onto her seat, then turned left onto 98 and headed for the bridge to Apalach. Outside her windows, the bay gleamed like a newly-polished mirror, tinted a rich yellow from the late afternoon sun.

⚓ ⚓ ⚓

She pulled up in front of the hotel about ten minutes later, just in time to see Dwight hurry out of the office with a young blond woman in tow. Maggie didn't know her, but she was wearing a maid's smock. She looked a little upset. Dwight looked significantly more upset.

"What are you doing?" Maggie asked, as she got out of the Cherokee.

"Well, I was sitting over there in the parking lot when Carrie here came out to her car, getting ready to leave for the day," Dwight said. "Carrie's my Mom's next door neighbor."

Maggie glanced at her just long enough to acknowledge her, then looked back at Dwight. "Okay," she prompted.

"Well, she knew I was doing *somethin'* cause she saw me sitting out here earlier," Dwight said. "So I told her I was waiting on our guy. Only she says he left this morning, before I even got here. Must have been right after you had Linda check on him."

"Oh, crap."

"Yeah. I've been sitting here all day surveilling nothing," he said. "Linda just let me in, and he's gone."

"Crap, crap," Maggie said again. "He's got a boat. I think it's here."

"A boat? You think—"

"Can I go on home?" the blond girl asked.

"Yeah, go ahead," Maggie said, waving her off. As the girl walked toward the parking lot, Maggie looked back at Dwight. "It's a Bertram Mark 3. A cruiser named *Rapture*. Clearly, it's not here. You check over at Scipio Creek, since it's closest. I'm going to try Ten Foot Hole. I'll call it in on the way."

"He's had all damn day to get gone," Dwight said.

Maggie shook her head. "He's got a meeting set up for sometime today or tonight, out on the water."

"Reckon that's why he's stuck around?"

"I'm sure it's one reason," she answered as she climbed back into the Jeep.

She had just started the engine and put it into reverse when Dwight ran up to her window, holding out his cell phone. "It's Mike. Says he's been trying to call you."

Maggie put the Jeep back in park and took the phone from him. "Hey, Mike."

"Your phone's dead."

"I know. What's up?" She put the phone on speaker so Dwight could hear.

"The cigarette butt you got off of Mann. It's a match for the other butts from the dock. Still gonna have to send them off to Tallahassee for DNA—"

"Mike, I have to go, but thank you," Maggie said hurriedly, then hung up and handed Dwight his phone. "Go to Scipio. If you find the boat, you call it in and wait for back up, you hear me?"

"Yeah," Dwight said, and turned to leave.

"Dwight!"

"Back up," Dwight said over his shoulder.

Maggie backed out before picking up her dash radio. "Franklin 100 to Franklin," she said.

"Go ahead, Franklin 100," the dispatcher said.

"I need a BOLO for a boat," Maggie answered. A Bertram Mark 3, boat's name is *Rapture*. Registration number Foxtrot-Lima-five-seven-nine-three-Alpha-Foxtrot. Boat belongs to homicide suspect Tobias Mann." Maggie didn't need to specify which homicide; they only had the one.

"10-4, Franklin 100," the dispatcher responded.

"Franklin 106 is on his way to Scipio Creek and I'm headed over to Ten Foot Hole," Maggie continued.

"10-4 Franklin 100."

Maggie hung up her handset and pulled onto Market Street.

CHAPTER
TWENTY-ONE

T en Foot Hole was a small city marina located across the street from Battery Park, just beneath the John Gorrie Bridge. The boat launch was popular with locals taking their small craft out for the day, and cruisers headed south frequently moored for the day to go exploring downtown. It had also been Maggie's husband David's home for the last year of his life.

Maggie had sold his old, 38-foot Burns Craft houseboat for a few thousand less than she could have, only because the couple planned to have it hauled over to Port St. Joe. Not having to see the boat every time she drove by was worth a few thousand to Maggie. She'd added the money she did get to the small life insurance policy she'd split between the two kids' college funds.

Maggie pulled around to the large gravel parking area near the boat launch on the Water Street side. As she did, she saw Mel Drummond walking to his old Nissan pickup. Mel had been living on his sailboat there for at least a few years. He and David had frequently played gin rummy on one deck or the other.

Maggie rolled down her window. "Hey, Mel!"

Mel looked over at her and smiled, his dentures whiter than his hair, his round cheeks permanently reddened by salt and sun. "Hey there, Maggie," he said. "I'm heading over to Lynn's to get some oysters. Wanna eat?"

Maggie got out of the car and glanced around the L-shaped marina. There were quite a few boats in, people headed south for warmer waters. They made it hard to look for one boat in particular, especially one she didn't know.

"No, thanks, Mel," she said. "Hey, I'm looking for a boat. A cruiser."

"What kind?" he asked as he opened his door. It screamed a protest on its rusty hinges.

"A Bertram Mark 3," she answered. She was going to try to explain what that was, but Mel smiled widely.

"Yeah, I know it," he said. "Fella pulled it in last week. Been here ever since with a busted hose, but Wadley's finally came out yesterday and fixed her up."

Maggie's heartbeat quickened "Is it still here?"

"Yeah, right over there," he answered. He turned and pointed across the marina to the long dock on the Bay Avenue side. "Right there. The one over there in Slip 9, with the flybridge."

"Okay, thanks, Mel," Maggie said, and closed the door of the Jeep.

"Everything okay?" Mel called. Maggie smiled and waved him off, and he carefully climbed into his truck and started it up. Maggie walked a little bit closer to the boat ramp and squinted across the water. It was dusk, the marina wasn't particularly well-lit, and she was too far away to tell if anyone was on the deck of the Bertram.

She was about to walk back to the Cherokee and call in when movement on the far dock caught her eye. She took a few steps to the side to get a clearer view around a small ketch. It took a moment for her to be sure, but it was Mann, headed for the Bertram. She hurried back to the Jeep, reached through the open window, and keyed her handset.

"Franklin 100 to Franklin."

"Go ahead, Franklin 100," the dispatcher answered.

"I've located the boat at Ten Foot Hole, Bay Avenue side. Homicide suspect Toby Mann is on site. Have all units looking for subject meet me at this location. Standing by for back-up."

"10-4. All units, subject boat and suspect have been located at Ten Foot Hole in Zone 1," the dispatcher said. "All available units please be 10-51 to Franklin 100's 10-20."

Maggie heard Dwight respond immediately. "Franklin 104 10-51," he said.

A few seconds later, Maggie heard Wyatt's voice. "Franklin 102 10-51."

This was followed immediately by a response from Apalach PD. "607 10-51 to that location." Maggie recognized Richard Chase, a young patrolman who lived down the road from her parents.

Her radio still crackling with responses, Maggie replaced the hand set and headed for the grassy area that fronted the marina. She'd love to take the Jeep and have her radio with her since her phone was dead, but Toby Mann knew her vehicle.

She stopped about halfway across the front of the marina, at a small picnic shelter, and looked toward the boat again. She couldn't see Toby. He'd gone aboard while she was on the radio. She huffed out a sigh and walked over to the foot of the dock, then looked all the way down.

The boat was docked with the bow facing Maggie, and after a moment, she saw Toby come out a side door from the salon and walk toward the bow. Listening below and beyond traffic noise and the tinny racket of a little outboard heading in, Maggie could now discern the sound of a much more powerful diesel engine. Mann jumped onto the dock and bent to loosen his bow line. He was leaving.

"Crap," Maggie whispered to herself, and was withdrawing her service weapon when Mann jumped back aboard, dropped his line sloppily onto the deck, and straightened up. Then something else caused her heart to slam against her ribs.

There was someone rising up on the flybridge above Mann. Maggie held her Glock 23 at her side and started down the dock. As Mann turned his back to Maggie, the figure on the flybridge jumped down on top of him. It was fast, very fast, and both men landed hard on the deck, but Maggie knew who it was. She started running.

Maggie was halfway to the boat when she heard a metallic rattling, and saw Axel stand up, pulling Toby to his knees from behind.

"Axel!" Maggie yelled, but he didn't even turn to look. "Axel!"

As she ran, Axel dragged Toby toward the portside gunwale. Axel had something around the other man's neck, and when Toby splayed his legs and spun halfway around, struggling to get free, Maggie saw that it was a length of chain. Two seconds later, Axel tossed Toby over the side. Toby's feet kicked at the water as Axel, and the chain, held him up against the boat by hs bulging neck.

Maggie had a good ten yards left to go. She called Axel's name again, but he either ignored her or didn't hear. Her voice was probably drowned out by the sirens of the cruisers that were screaming into the parking area. Maggie wanted to look, but didn't take her eyes from Axel.

He was focused on Toby, who was grabbing at the chain around his neck and kicking his legs.

"How does that feel, buddy?" Axel asked, his voice strained. His biceps bulged beneath his worn blue tee shirt. "What's it like?"

Maggie stumbled to a stop just a few feet away. "Axel, stop it! Let him go!"

Axel looked up at her and said something, but his voice was low, and she couldn't make it out. Toby was making all kinds of noise; wet, strangled noises from his throat, and the dull thud of his feet against the boat.

"Axel, I need you to let him go or pull him up!" she said, raising her weapon without any inclination to use it. She could hear hard soles thumping up the dock, more than one pair of them. She glanced over her shoulder and saw Richard, followed closely by Dwight. There were more men further back on the dock, but she didn't take the time to see who.

She looked back at Axel, and saw that he'd seen the officers, too. He didn't seem to care; he just looked back down at Toby, his face almost as red as Toby's from the effort of holding him there. Shrimpers were some of the strongest men Maggie knew, but Toby had to weight about one-sixty, and Axel wasn't just letting him dangle; he was tightening the chain as well.

Maggie raised her weapon higher as Richard ran behind her and stopped a few feet to her right, assumed a shooting stance, and levelled his weapon. She could see Dwight do the same on her left, but she didn't look.

"Axel, drop him, man!" Dwight shouted.

Axel looked up at them, his cheeks puffing outward, his neck turning red, but he didn't say anything back.

"Blackwell, come on!" Richard yelled, sounding very worried that he might have to follow through with something he had no desire to do at all.

"Axel, look at me!" Maggie yelled. He did. "Somebody is going to shoot you, and if you make it me I will never forgive you! Do you hear me?"

Axel looked at her for a moment, as Toby's eyes wandered off in the direction of his frontal lobe. Then he let go with both hands, and Toby and the chain fell the foot or so into the water. Maggie took her first breath in what felt like minutes, as Richard laid down on the dock, reached out, and grabbed Toby, who was torn between sinking and struggling.

Maggie heard heavy footfalls behind her, then Wyatt appeared next to Richard and helped him haul Toby into the dock. Dwight holstered his weapon and pulled out a pair of cuffs. Maggie looked back at Axel, as he stepped lightly onto the dock in front of her, breathing hard. She stared at him as he got his breath.

She barely heard Dwight reading Toby his rights, or Richard calling for a paramedic unit. She only vaguely saw Wyatt jump aboard to shut off the engine. She grabbed the sleeve of Axel's shirt and pulled him toward her as she walked a few feet back up the dock. She stopped just beyond the bow and turned to face him.

"How did you find him?"

"I followed you. Then I followed him."

"You should have called me," she said.

He looked fairly apologetic, but he looked even more sad. "If it had been the guy that killed David, would you have called it in?"

Maggie felt heat rising in her chest, coating the surface of her eyes. She blinked, was about to say something then, without knowing she would do it, lifted her foot to his belly and pushed him off the dock

⚓ ⚓ ⚓

It was full dark by the time the paramedics had given Toby a quick once-over, then hauled him off to the ER. Sheriff Curtis Bledsoe had appeared on the scene, hoping the news would show up eventually. They hadn't.

He'd heard about Axel's involvement over the police radio, and had announced his intention to charge him with assault and obstruction and who knew what else, until Maggie mentioned that Toby had attacked Axel, not the other way around. She didn't look at Axel when she said it, but she felt him looking at her. She felt Wyatt looking, too.

With no photo opps available, Bledsoe had just taken his leave. Maggie sat at the picnic shelter, downing the last of a bottle of water. Across the street, Axel was smoking as he leaned against Dwight's cruiser. Dwight was still telling him how pissed his mama would have been at him if he'd shot Axel, who was her favorite pupil in the fourth grade.

Wyatt walked over to Maggie and sat down heavily beside her on the bench, mammoth Mountain Dew in hand. She glanced over at him, then looked at the ground.

"Don't sweat it," Wyatt said. "Once he can speak again, I think this guy will be hesitant to accuse Axel of anything. Clearly, Axel is a hometown boy."

Maggie looked over at him. "It just came out," she said quietly.

"Well, it's said. Can't unsay it."

Maggie sighed and thumped her empty water bottle against her knee. "I'm becoming a lousy cop."

Wyatt was quiet for a moment. "No. It's just that Maggie is your dominant side, not Lt. Redmond."

"Is that good or bad?"

He frowned down at her, but his look was more concern than reproach. "It's both."

Maggie looked back down at the dirt, heard Wyatt take a swallow of his soda.

"For the record, if it had been you, if I had been in Axel's shoes, I would have done the same," he said finally. Maggie looked up at him. "But I'd have let him get the boat out on the water first." Maggie stared at him as he screwed the cap back on his bottle. "Genius, my ass."

CHAPTER
TWENTY-TWO

Two days later, Maggie walked out of The Shop, on the corner of Avenue D and Commerce, just a block from Water Street and Riverfront Park. She tucked a small bag into her purse, pulled out her keys, and squinted into the morning light as she took a drink of her coffee. Extra shot, no cardboard.

A familiar truck turned the corner from Water Street and stopped. "Hey," Axel called out his window.

She raised a hand, and he backed up a little, then pulled into a space across the street. When he got out and started crossing the street toward her, she had to blink once or twice.

He was wearing khaki pants and a navy blazer. A maroon and gold striped tie hung untied from the collar of a white button-down shirt. The clothes were enough of an anomaly, but the strangest thing was seeing him without a ball cap. The morning breeze was a strong one, and it blew his brown hair straight up and then down into his eyes. As he stepped onto the sidewalk, she resisted the urge to fix it for him.

"Hey," she said.

"Hey."

"It's Mari's memorial today?"

"Yeah," he answered. He eyed her coffee cup. "Can I get a sip of that?"

Maggie handed him the cup and watched him drink. "Is that David's tie?" she asked softly.

He nodded, his eyes darting to the sidewalk. "I borrowed it for that Seafood Workers' banquet a couple years ago," he said, and she saw him swallow hard. "I've forgotten how to operate the damn thing."

Maggie stepped closer and pulled the two ends into place, started tying it for him. They were quiet for a moment.

Every day of her young life, there had been the three of them. She and her best friend David and David and his best friend Axel. There had seldom been two of them without the third. Now, every time she and Axel were together, there was a David-shaped hole there with them. It sucked unspoken words into itself like a vacuum.

"I'm off today," she said. "Do you want me to come with you?"

Axel shrugged one shoulder and shook his head. "I got it."

She finished his knot, then took back her coffee and sipped it, just for something to do besides feel awkward and unhelpful.

When she looked up, he was staring over at Riverfront Park. The place where they'd both watched David die. The breeze ruffled his hair again, and there was something sweet and soft about the way it made him appear. She left it alone.

"I love you, Axel," she said

He met her eye for just a moment, then focused somewhere beyond her. "Ditto, Mag-lite."

Maggie hadn't heard him call her that in decades. She couldn't even remember why he'd started.

Then he grabbed her hand, quickly squeezed the tips of her fingers, and walked away. She watched him go, watched him turn left toward 98 and Tampa and regret. Once he was gone, she was alone on the small block. It was just her, the wind, and one lone pelican perched on a piling at the park.

She hadn't been there in months, not since David had died. She had even changed coffee places, because Café con Leche looked out on the park, and she couldn't bear to see it every day. There was a time when it had been one of her favorite places in town, with its small strip of grass, iron benches, and two or three old shrimp boats at a time.

She found herself standing on the grass before she'd noticed she was walking. She took a deep breath in through her nose, smelled the briny sharpness of Scipio Creek, felt the cool air calm and soothe her. The pelican regarded her for a moment, then flapped his great wings and flew off in that slow motion only pelicans and cranes seem able to employ.

She watched him go, and smiled.

⚓ ⚓ ⚓

Maggie pulled open the glass door of the Sheriff's Office, waved at Vera the receptionist, and started down the hall. Terry Coyle, the other investigator for the department, stopped short outside the break room when he saw her.

"Hey, Mags, what are you doing here?"

"Nothing," she said, shrugging, and hurried past him.

She rounded the corner to the back hall and almost walked in to Dwight.

"Hey, uh, Maggie," he said as she passed him. "I thought you were off."

"Nothing," she said over her shoulder. She was starting to feel nervous, and she waited for Dwight to round the corner, then she stopped, took a deep breath, and continued on to Wyatt's door, which was open, as usual. She walked in and shut the door behind her, leaned against it.

Wyatt was sitting at his computer, poking away at some public relations document or another. He looked up and smiled, then started to stand.

She held up a hand. "Don't move," she said, and was annoyed when her voice broke.

He stopped mid-stand and looked at her, then sat back down. "Ok. Aren't you off today?"

"Don't speak," Maggie said.

"Okay," he said. "Can I just say 'okay'?"

"Please shut up," she said.

"Okay."

He waited, his brows knitting together over his nose. Maggie took a deep breath and let it out slowly.

"Are you being chased?" he asked her.

"Shut up," she said quietly. He did, and waited. It took Maggie a moment to speak. "I have been really blessed. To have two best friends in my life. David was my best friend. You're my best friend."

He looked like he might speak, so she held her hand up again. He stopped looking like that.

"I want…I want to take care of you. I want you to take care of me. I want to make you sandwiches, and make you laugh the way you make me laugh, and just…be the place you go when you need to know how important you are."

Maggie's eyes started to heat and she blinked a few times to clear them. "I know I loved David. I loved him for forever, and I loved him very much. But I wasn't in love with him. He didn't make me nervous or make me mad or make me feel this…urgency in my stomach every time I saw him. I only feel like that with you."

She blew out a breath and took a few steps toward the desk, then stopped. Wyatt's face was unreadable, something that didn't happen often.

"I know I'm a pain, and I'm damaged and closed off and all kinds of less than ideal things, but I promise you that I love you more than I ever realized was possible." Her throat felt dry and sticky, and she tried and failed to swallow.

"Will you marry me, Wyatt?"

He looked at her a moment, and she wondered why her heart was beating so hard. They had talked about this. This was not a surprise. It was all okay. And sometimes change was scary, but good.

She was about to repeat the question when he shrugged one shoulder. "Yeah, sure," he said simply, then turned back to his computer. She stood there for a second until he started jabbing at the keyboard again, then she spun around and headed for the door. She only made it two steps before she heard his chair squeak.

"Wait a minute, you little idiot!" he said behind her, and she heard laughter in his voice. One huge hand plopped onto her shoulder as she jerked the door open. The other one reached out and pushed the door shut again. She turned back around and glared up at him.

"I'm sorry!" he said, and she wanted to slap the grin right out from under his moustache. "I couldn't resist, it was like the best straight line you've ever given me."

"You're an ass!" she said.

"I know, but we're gonna get married anyway," he said. His smile grew warmer, less mirthful. "I'm sorry. Yes. Of course."

"Why do you have to be a jerk?" she asked, as she looked down and fumbled in her purse. "I'm glad I just got you this crappy shell ring."

"You got me a ring?" he asked as she pulled out the little bag from The Shop.

"Well, I didn't know if I was supposed to. I mean, I'm the one proposing. It's confusing."

"That's so cute," he said, as she pulled out the ring, a creamy color with swirls of pale orange.

"It's a shell ring," she said.

"I know. You told me."

She held the ring out on her palm. "Well, here. And quit looming."

"I'm not looming," he snapped only slightly, as he took the ring.

He tried it on his ring finger, but it didn't go past his first knuckle, despite the fact that Maggie had dug through the entire box to find the biggest one. He slipped it onto his pinkie instead.

"You don't have to wear it," Maggie said. "It's just a symbol."

"I'll wear it," he said gently.

"Okay," Maggie said to his chest. "I don't need an engagement ring. I never had one with David. We can just get wedding bands."

"You can't make all of the decisions just because you proposed," he said mildly as he turned and walked over to his desk. "I gave you permission to propose."

"You gave me permission—" she started as he leaned over his desk and opened a drawer.

"You're welcome," he said over his shoulder. Then he turned and walked back to her, a small pale blue box in his hand.

"What's that?" she asked him.

He opened the box to reveal a delicate silver ring with a small, square aquamarine stone.

"It was my Mom's," he said quietly. "She sent it to me to give you."

Maggie looked up at Wyatt. "When?"

"June."

"June?!"

"I told you you were lagging behind me," he said quietly.

When she looked up at him, he looked her square in the eye, and his gaze was warm and kind and lacking even a hint of humor. "She wants us to have it," he said.

Maggie swallowed, then looked down at her hand as Wyatt lifted it, then slipped the ring on her finger. It was slightly big, but they could fix that.

"Wow, we're really going to do it," she said as she looked up at him.

"Yeah," he said quietly, then leaned down and kissed her gently on the lower lip. He straightened and smiled at her for a moment, then patted her head.

"So, that's that, then," he said.

A FEW WORDS OF THANKS

I hope you've enjoyed reading *Apparent Wind*. If you'd be kind enough to leave an honest review, I'd be most appreciative. You can also sign up for my mailing list to be notified when the next book in the series is available. You can also follow my Facebook page. We have a pretty good time over there.

I owe so many people so much, for their help, support and encouragement. Thank you to Debbie Maxwell Allen for her patience and lack of sighing while editing this book. Many warm thanks to Colleen Sheehan of Write Dream Repeat book design for the always gorgeous interior design and typesetting, and to Shayne Rutherford of Dark Moon Graphics for yet another beautiful cover.

Thank you to John Solomon, formerly of the Franklin County Sheriff's Office and now the Apalachicola Chamber of Commerce, for his willingness to answer questions, correct technical mistakes, and sign books for readers. He's a star; go see him when you're in town.

Thanks, as always, to my dear friends and fellow authors in The Group That Shall Not Be Named, for their unfailing support, humor, and reality checks. Y'all are something else entirely.

To my family, particularly my Mom and my amazing kids; you inspire and motivate me daily. Thank you for helping me live my dream.

Finally, thank you to you guys—you beautiful readers— for sticking with me through delays and broken promises and the occasional asteroid. Your emails and Facebook posts are a constant source of laughter, warmth, and encouragement. I could write another book about how much every single one of you means to me.

CPSIA information can be obtained
at www.ICGtesting.com
Printed in the USA
LVOW10s2321010217
522952LV00006B/116/P